Library at Home Service
Community Services
Hounslow Library, CentreSpace
24 Treaty Centre, High Street
Hounslow TW3 1ES

WORKING IN PARTNERSHIP WITH

0	1	2	3	4	5	6	7	8	9
890	979	7583			565	7726	9587	1588	9509
9810		8283	364			706	1927	268	
7670	972		9623			6306		808	
	611		3078 9534				3087 1978		
	861		9744				507	268	
			943				9977		
	901								
		9913							
	0771								

P10-L2061

HER HEART'S DESIRE

Viscount John Coombe is forbidden by his war disabled father to fight Napoleon, and is told to marry. Soon after John meets Felicity, her maid steals her precious necklace and takes it abroad. John grasps the opportunity to go and search for it, taking Felicity and her aunts so that no one will suspect he is on government business. Felicity begins to wonder if John really loves her. Was his offer of marriage a mere convenience?

Books by Anne Holman
in the Linford Romance Library:

SAIL AWAY TO LOVE

ANNE HOLMAN

HER HEART'S DESIRE

Complete and Unabridged

LINFORD
Leicester

First published in Great Britain

First Linford Edition
published 1998

British Library CIP Data

Holman, Anne
    Her heart's desire.—Large print ed.—
Linford romance library
1. Love stories
2. Large type books
I. Title
823.9'14 [F]

ISBN 0–7089–5361–1

Published by
F. A. Thorpe (Publishing) Ltd.
Anstey, Leicestershire
Set by Words & Graphics Ltd.
Anstey, Leicestershire
Printed and bound in Great Britain by
T. J. International Ltd., Padstow, Cornwall

This book is printed on acid-free paper

1

Brilliant candles from the chandeliers lit the London ballroom. Ladies' jewels and the gold braid on scarlet uniforms sparkled as dancers whirled to the lilting dance music.

In the pause between dances, John, Viscount Coombe, attired in a dark blue coat, white waistcoat, black knee breeches, and an expertly-tied cravat, grimaced as he shifted his weight from one silver-buckled shoe to the other trying to make up his mind which of the giggly, young ladies he should ask to partner him for the next dance.

The Season's prettiest girls were already engaged, but many plainer young ladies seated by the ballroom wall were considering him hopefully.

He decided he had endured more than enough. He had danced with a dozen or more simpering, young ladies.

Surely it was time for him to go and relish a quiet brandy at home?

But, his conscience warned him, he would never obtain a wife — or more importantly, an heir — if he gave up this opportunity to meet a suitable female.

He sighed. He feared that at the age of thirty-five he was too old for any of those white-gowned maidens, although he was well aware many mothers were angling to catch him, an eligible and wealthy viscount, as a husband for their young daughter.

It annoyed him to think that he could excel in practically every gentleman's occupation he chose to do — but when it came to meeting a suitable woman, he baulked.

He suspected it was because he was unfamiliar with female company. His commanding father, the Earl of Wanstead, had shunned ladies after his wife died.

He also blamed the old earl for forbidding his son and heir to take a commission, and fight Napoleon like the rest of the young men of his acquaintance.

As the orchestra struck up, the viscount turned to leave the ballroom. Before he approached those pale muslins again, he would fortify himself with a glass of wine.

Weaving between the high-pitched, chattering guests he headed for the ante-room where the refreshments were laid out.

Beckoning a footman to hand him a glass of wine, he sipped the ruby liquid thankfully. His eyes meandered around the room. Yes, he recognised most of the ton present, many of whom he preferred to avoid meeting.

Envy hit him as he saw pretty girls fluttering around resplendently-uniformed soldiers boasting of their adventures in the Peninsula War. He was in sombre evening dress, and had no entertaining stories to tell.

Strolling out of the refreshment room he wandered into the less crowded grand hall. A quieter place to relish his drink. The wine began to mellow his thoughts towards his father, Earl Wanstead, and his order to do his duty: find a wife and beget an heir.

As he raised his glass once more he felt something light roll over his highly-polished evening slipper, and looking down, saw a small, round bottle bowling along the black and white tiled flooring.

'Oh, I beg your pardon, sir. The smelling salts slipped out of my hand.'

A woman's low and sensuous voice made John start. Turning to seek the owner of the enchanting voice he was startled to find himself facing a trio of plainly-dressed, older ladies. Seated in a row in a dark alcove under the stairs they peered out at him like birds from their nest.

The viscount picked up the runaway bottle and bowed stiffly before holding it out, enquiring, 'Your property, ma'am?'

'Thank you, sir,' one of the matrons

twittered, her curled ostrich feathers doing a little dance over her head as she spoke. However, she made no effort to take the offered vial.

The viscount turned to the next grey lady sitting beside her.

'Then, it is yours, ma'am?'

'Give it to Felicity,' she said, nodding at the third lady.

Obediently, John turned to look at the last female.

As he offered the small bottle of salts to her he was amazed to find the hand that took it was well-shaped and as smooth as silk.

'Thank you, sir,' the charming contralto voice sounded again.

John blinked. With growing interest he studied the small, bespectacled face of the lady with the beautiful voice. He was mistaken, she was not old, although she was dressed as though she might be wearing older ladies' cast-off clothes.

Indeed, she was not anything much to look at — but he noticed her eyes twinkled intelligently behind those severe eyeglasses — reminding him of a caged animal longing to escape.

'Hmm,' his lordship said, unusually at a loss for words.

Here was a mysterious female who fascinated him at this accursed ball.

'Hmm,' he said again, thinking, as he studied the younger lady hiding in the gloom, I wonder why this female is being disguised as someone far older.

As he watched her slip the smelling salts into her reticule, he knew he could leave, but an inner urge to stay with the lady who had intrigued him made him say, 'I believe you have had no supper, ladies. May I fetch some refreshments for you?'

This suggestion seemed to please the older, plumper ladies especially.

'Felicity, please go and see if you can assist the . . . the gentleman,' the lady with the ostrich feather ordered.

He was surprised the older ladies treated Felicity as a companion, telling her to go with him, and did not consider it necessary for her to have a chaperone. But then, unflatteringly attired as she was, did she need one?

'Let me introduce myself. My name is Coombe. Er, John,' the viscount said as his tall figure bowed — feeling as he knew the young lady's name, she should know his. His name did not appear to ring a bell with them. They were obviously not familiar with the highest circles of society.

'And we, sir, are the Misses Ward. These are my aunts, Sophie and Jane. And I am Miss Felicity Ward.'

The young lady had risen with such alacrity, he suspected the poor girl had been kept under by the older ladies for far too long. Felicity curtsied prettily, and John gallantly offered her his arm.

There was something graceful in her walk that made her easy to guide, and made up for the fact that she was probably the worst-dressed young lady at the ball.

'There's a sad crush here,' the

viscount commented as he skilfully escorted her through the crowd towards the food tables.

'With you I feel I shall not be crushed,' she replied in her mellow voice, and her comment flattered him.

Felicity, looking at the well-shaped features of this dauntingly competent gentleman, decided his soft grey eyes and well-formed lips should be enticed into a smile. But his attention was on hailing a footman to serve them.

'Now, ma'am, what can I get you to eat and drink?'

'May I choose for my aunts, sir, as I know what they like?'

'Indeed. And for yourself?' His dark eyebrows rose sharply to demand she tell him her preferences — if she had ever been allowed any.

'Oh, I'm happy to eat what they have,' she answered good-naturedly.

'But not as much,' he replied, viewing her slender figure with the quick smile she had been hoping for. Her gurgle of laughter had the effect of making his usually straight mouth curve at the sides.

Behind her unfortunate appearance he detected a star-like glimmer of spirit. And, looking carefully down at her, he noticed a beautiful sapphire necklace around her creamy, slender neck that twinkled with her lively brown eyes under her glasses.

At some time this well-bred girl must have had better means than she has now, he reasoned.

'Well, tonight, Miss Ward, I insist you choose to eat what you fancy,' he informed her.

'Thank you, sir.' She gave him an irresistible smile that made him grin.

Like the sun coming out and shining on him, John immediately felt more relaxed. For the first time that evening he felt happy. Felicity was soon engaged making sure that her fastidious aunts were going to be satisfied with what she chose for them.

'I think you are overlooking your platter,' the viscount reminded her as his long arms came in useful to stretch over to reach the cuts of cold meats, salads, breads and jellies.

'Oh, please, put anything on my plate — it all looks so delicious,' Felicity replied.

Viscount Coombe had the impression the young lady was easy to please. And it made him feel good to think that this evening he had helped to give a treat to a non-complaining, downtrodden young woman.

'Drinks?' he enquired.

'Lemonade is what they like.'

'And you? No, don't answer, Miss Ward. I know your answer will be that you will be satisfied with lemonade, too. But let me tempt you into having a glass of wine.'

'Well, I must admit I don't particularly like cordials.'

Felicity gave him another beaming smile that made him almost drop a plate in sheer delight at the warmth of it.

She was nothing much to look at in

those ill-assorted clothes, but her smile and voice pleased him more than he could imagine!

Two footmen had been pressed into service by the viscount. One carried a small table, the other balanced a trayload with four filled platters. Felicity followed, carrying a smaller tray with the glasses or lemonade.

The viscount, who was delighted he had managed to acquire a bottle of the same excellent wine he had relished earlier, and two wine glasses, led the way through the crowd back into the hall.

'Gracious!' Aunt Sophie exclaimed, waving her hat feather excitedly, 'You have brought us a veritable feast!'

'Indeed it is,' Aunt Jane endorsed, giving him a quick nod of satisfaction. 'And I can enjoy it as my headache has quite gone.'

'We hope it satisfies,' his lordship murmured, pleased by their approval as he organised the footmen to place the table and trays of food and drinks comfortably close to the ladies.

'Now we are short of a chair,' Felicity commented dismayed, as she looked around with no hope whatsoever of finding one. But the viscount darted off and soon returned with a footman bearing one aloft. Felicity was impressed by his competence.

The ladies were clearly highly delighted to have acquired a handsome male companion, as they enjoyed the refreshments he had procured for them.

'Do you ladies live in London?' John asked suddenly feeling he wanted to know more about them.

'Indeed, sir, we have a small house in Kensington,' Aunt Sophie replied. 'And do you, sir, reside in London?'

The viscount swallowed. It would not do to intimidate the ladies by telling them he had more than one house.

'I'm residing here at present,' he replied.

'And may we ask you what is your

line of business, sir?'

John smiled, amused to think they thought him a tradesman.

'Oh, ma'am, I sometimes wonder myself!'

The two older ladies exchanged glances, and Aunt Sophie said, 'We can be sure he is successful — whatever he does. I would say you are a banker. What do you think, Jane?'

To the viscount's amusement, Aunt Jane studied him carefully.

'Now let me guess. With his charming manners I suspect you are a physician, sir?'

He shook his head of tousled brown hair.

'Alas, I cannot boast that my occupation has any use to society.'

John was enjoying both the game, and the praise, and felt a stab of surprise that women's company could be so entertaining.

'And what do you think, Felicity?' Aunt Jane asked her.

He was aware that Felicity was more

discerning than her aunts and was not surprised when she answered.

'I think . . . he is an adventurer!'

'You mean he travels to wild places?' Aunt Jane gulped.

Felicity's eyes twinkled.

'No, but I think he would like to!'

'You are a perceptive woman!' he said, winking at her.

He noticed she coloured, but as a true lady would, merely smiled pleasantly and continued with her meal.

John did not want to embarrass the ladies by telling them his rank, and changed the subject. As they continued supping, the ladies talked, laughed and thanked him warmly for taking care of them all which pleased him immensely.

There was only one problem, he thought as he chewed and swallowed, before downing the last of his wine. He was supposed to be finding a wife from the bevy of young girls.

Not sitting here under the staircase, enjoying himself supping with three amusing ladies — all of whom were on the shelf.

But he was enjoying himself so much, he really didn't feel like returning to the ballroom, and having to ask one of those silly chits to stand up with him. He suddenly held his breath . . . he couldn't ask plain Felicity to dance . . . in that unflattering gown . . . or could he?

Well, he might not have had the chance to show his bravery on the battlefield, but he was not without courage, and by God, if he felt comfortable in the company of this young lady, then hang the lot of them. He would dance with her!

He was not surprised to find people staring at them as they took the dance floor, nor that Felicity danced like an angel.

2

As her young maid brushed her hair
that night, Felicity still felt a glow of
pleasure that the ball had given her
— and especially the tall, intriguing
gentleman who had partnered her for
three heavenly dances.

She knew it was just by chance
that she had met John. And her
commonsense told her that she would
never see this prince of her dreams
again.

She did not normally move in circles
where she would meet gentlemen of
his class and had only attended that
one ball because she and her aunts
had received the invitation from an
old family friend.

Felicity had been blessed with a
sensible nature. She was well aware
that she had a plainish face, and that
she not only had to wear eyeglasses

much of the time, but had passed the first flush of youth. She was resigned to accepting that at the age of twenty-seven, marriage was unlikely to come her way. She knew there were many beautiful, rich, young ladies out to attract the eligible men. What chance had she, a poor, less fortunately endowed woman got against them?

But Felicity never wasted time bemoaning her lot. She was not unhappy living with her aunts. And she was far better off as their companion than being in the position of some ill-used governesses and companions she'd met.

Since the death of her parents and consequently the loss of her home, all her father's wealth had gone to her brother, Augustus, and his grasping wife. Felicity had been left with practically nothing to live on.

'Your sister has been born with a face no girl would choose to own. Anyway, she is far too old to marry now, Augustus, and will not require her dowry,' Beatrice, her sister-in-law, told him, thinking the money could be put to good use for a new wing to their already extensive house. 'I think you should arrange for her to make her home with your aunts — they can afford to provide all she will need.'

Augustus, pompous, and now wealthy, who also showed little sympathy for his older sister's plight, was happy to pay his aunts a very small sum to keep her.

The only thing of value Felicity was permitted to keep was her sapphire necklace which had belonged to her mama. She now unclasped it and handed it to the maid to place in its satin-lined leather case.

'This necklace must be very valuable, ma'am,' Bet mused, her face agog as she held up the necklace so that the cobalt sapphires blazed and shimmered in the candlelight.

'Indeed it is, Bet. But as far as I'm concerned, it is its sentimental value that is important to me — you see it is the only thing I have that belonged to my dear mama.'

The maid took a last look at it before closing the jewel box and then she walked across the room to place it safely in the drawer where Felicity always kept it.

It never occurred to Felicity that the very next day, both Bet, and her necklace, would disappear.

★ ★ ★

Felicity had just made the terrible discovery, when another surprise hit her. John had come on a morning visit. Dabbing her red eyes, and thankful her eye-glasses would hide the evidence that she had been weeping, Felicity dressed herself without the help of a maid, and went down to the parlour.

What has made him come, she wondered, as she stepped down the stairs.

All she could think of was that he possessed good manners, and paying

19

them a visit after the ball was a courtesy they could expect from a fine young man like him. Unfortunately, in her present sad state she could not feel elated.

Seeing the tall, broad-shouldered visitor rise and bow to greet her made Felicity forget everything but him. Her heart beat faster remembering how they'd danced and laughed together last night, and yet this morning it was all she could do to wish good morning to this handsome, well-dressed gentleman.

'You took so long coming we thought we were never going to see you, Felicity,' Aunt Sophie scolded, who did not appear in the least put out to have a man of his calibre to entertain.

Well, Felicity thought, if my aunts are not worried by his status neither should I be.

'Then you are fortunate to have had the pleasure of the gentleman's company far longer than I will, Aunt,' Felicity declared as she curtsied, determined to make the visitor smile. She was delighted to see that he did.

'The pleasure is mine,' he said as his grey eyes studied her for a seemingly long time. His smile was surprisingly sensuous and Felicity felt a surge of warmth come into her cheeks. 'I'm delighted to see you again.'

He certainly gave the impression he was genuinely pleased.

She admired his fashionable black coat, which he wore with the newstyle long trousers and lace-up shoes.

The warmth of his smile prevented her from feeling too overpowered dressed in her simple day gown, and the lack of luxury in the furnishings of their small parlour.

'Now Felicity is here, shall we go and make our shopping list, Jane?' Aunt Sophie said. The sisters rose and walked towards the parlour door. But not before John had got there first to open it for the two older ladies.

'Your aunts are delightful characters — and look very alike,' he said returning to sit opposite Felicity.

'Indeed, they are dears,' Felicity agreed, flattered that he was choosing to stay and talk to her — little knowing how at ease he felt in her company, and how much he enjoyed listening to her mellow voice. 'Aunt Sophie is inclined to be bossy, and has a long, inquisitive nose. Aunt Jane has a rounder face and is a little on the fussy side.'

'So I've observed.'

Felicity was not surprised he was sharp-eyed. She just hoped he hadn't noticed how badly she'd dressed her hair without the help of a maid. And how she was hiding her distress — but, she feared there was nothing she'd be able to hide for long from this alert gentleman.

And so she said, 'You must excuse me for being a little downcast this morning, sir. I awoke this morning to find my maid had run off with my . . . ' To her horror a trickle of tears started to run down her face. 'My sapphire necklace is gone.' She gulped trying to control her emotion.

John stood, crossed the room and sat on the sofa beside Felicity concerned obviously at her distressed countenance.

'I'm very sorry to hear this.'

Felicity felt herself flushing all over at having him so close. Hearing the sincerity in his voice, seeing the sympathy in his eyes, she tried her best not to give way to having a good cry.

'The necklace belonged to Mama, and it was the only thing of hers I had.'

John's large palm covered her trembling hands in a sudden intimacy.

'What are you doing to recover it?' he asked quietly.

Felicity pressed her lips together as she made the effort to overcome her vapours. Her voice sounded as though a frog was speaking.

'My aunts have not been told yet . . . but I fear they will be able to do nothing to recover it. Bet Murray, my maid, is very young, and I would have thought too witless to steal anything valuable. She has not been with me long.' She shook her head sorrowfully, unable to say more.

He cleared his throat.

'Unfortunately, one occasionally finds a dishonest servant. Perhaps your maid had an accomplice. Do you think you could tell me all you know about her, and I will make some enquiries for you?'

Felicity forgot she'd been trying to hide her tears and removed her glasses. Using her fingers she wiped her wet cheeks. He supplied her with a snowy white handkerchief.

Her vulnerability enchanted him. The poor weeping girl! He felt he would do anything to find her precious necklace.

She looked up, blinking back her tears. He actually seemed to be interested in the theft of her necklace. Of course, he would not be able to find the jewels, which were now probably in the less reputable area of London, being sold for the highest price Bet could get for them. But how kind of him to offer to help her!

Having told him all she knew of Bet Murray — which did not amount to much — she put her glasses back on and looked at him expectantly. It was amazing that in the short time she'd known him she felt she could trust him.

'Now, Felicity, what can you tell me about the necklace?'

'Well, my mother told me it came from my Dutch grandparents. I believe she said it had matching earrings, a 'suite set', I think they are called — but what became of the other pieces I do not know.'

Felicity thought her brother, who was a jeweller like her father had been, may know something more, but she felt disinclined to mention Augustus.

John whose eyes had been locked with hers for a few minutes, rubbed his chin.

'I can't promise you I'll find your necklace, but the sooner I start looking for it, then the better chance there is of finding it.'

'Where will you look?'

'You tell me Bet is young, therefore she must be working with a criminal. Maybe a relative, or a friend?'

'Why, yes, she did mention someone . . . Jake, I think his name was.'

'Ah! You see the pieces will fit together as I search and find them. I have a few contacts in the underworld. I shall go and look around for some more.'

'Why, thank you, sir!'

Felicity was both startled and delighted to think some effort was going to be made to find her family heirloom. And he seemed keen to do it. But then some gentlemen had plenty of time on their hands, although he did not seem the kind of man who would waste it.

Upon further reflection, she realised that he could mix with all classes. Unlike her brother, Augustus, he was not at all pompous. Yes, John would be able to disguise himself very easily, she considered. The thought occurred to her, too, that he would even consider the investigation fun!

'I appreciate your interest in my loss,' Felicity told him as she saw him out.

'Because the necklace means so much to you, I will do all I can to find it,' he replied as he looked down at her with a quick, encouraging smile. Then he bowed, and strode towards the door. Then he halted and swung around to say, 'I've left my card, and if you think of anything else that might assist the search for your necklace, please contact me.'

When he'd gone, Felicity went to the silver tray in the hall and picked up his visiting card, looking down at the name and address on it.

Viscount Coombe, it read.

Felicity's heart began to thump wildly. She'd never dreamed he was titled! But then, with his air, fine clothes and good manners, was she really surprised?

He had deliberately avoided telling them he was a viscount and she wondered why. But even stranger, she wondered why had he lowered himself to visit her. Had he perhaps enjoyed her company as much as she had enjoyed his last night? But even if they had danced well together it signified nothing.

She had neither beauty or standing to interest a gentleman of his high rank.

She told herself again that the viscount was merely being courteous coming to see her this morning after the ball. And if it were not for the fact that her maid had robbed her of one treasured possession — her mama's necklace — and she'd been clearly upset, then she doubted if he would have ever bothered himself about her in the future.

A quickening of her pulse made her gasp. She felt the loss of her jewellery was not necessarily the end of the world after all. She might never see her stolen necklace again — but she would be seeing the gentleman who had stolen her heart!

★ ★ ★

The Pool of London was thriving with trade. John found the place fascinating, and when visiting London frequently strolled around it exploring the area. The cargo boats of the British merchant fleet sailed to everywhere in the world.

He always dressed so as to be taken as a trader. No-one cast him a second look as he observed the imports of wine, brandy, sugar, coffee and tea arriving.

Keeping his eyes and ears open he also acquired interesting knowledge about the dockland folk. That morning he made his way to a district known for its shady dealings.

'Good day to you, Mr Perch,' the viscount said, removing his battered hat which had been discarded by his valet, as he entered a dingy little shop.

Mr Perch quickly removed a package to

under his counter and also endeavoured to hide his discomfort as a man slid out of the back of his shop.

'An' what can I do for you, sir?'

'A necklace, Mr Perch. I'm looking for a valuable, sapphire necklace. I hear you are the person with your ear to the ground about stolen merchandise.'

Mr Perch's pock-marked face twitched.

'I dunno about that necklace. I ain't got it.'

'Ah, Mr Perch, so you've heard about the necklace?'

'I might 'ave.'

His lordship took out his purse and laid a golden guinea on the counter. Then he placed another on the top of it.

'Well, now,' Mr Perch said rubbing his grubby hands together, 'now I come to think on it — I might 'ave 'eard something.'

The viscount added to the pile of gold pieces.

Mr Perch's eyes bulged and the information poured out of him.

'I heard about a cove, Jake, trying to sell them baubles, but as they was too hot for me — or anyone to handle, he set sail for Amsterdam with the early tide.'

'Ah! Did he now?' The viscount breathed with satisfaction. That would suit his plans admirably.

3

Sunshine and showers encouraged the spring bulbs to bloom. It heartened Felicity when she walked in the park and saw the flowers.

'I'm determined not to feel downcast, Aunt Jane,' she said to her companion. 'I'm confident Viscount Coombe will do all he can to retrieve my necklace.'

'Yes, I'm sure he will,' her aunt agreed, who was puffing slightly trying to keep up with her niece's lively footsteps.

'He's already sent me a message to say he will be visiting us again with some news, so he's not been lackadaisical about it either.'

'Felicity.' Aunt Jane halted and put her plump hand over her heaving bosom. 'We are out to take the air. Do not rush so.'

'I'm sorry to have hurried you, Aunt.

Shall we sit on this bench for a rest?'
Felicity smiled at her Aunt, pretending
she was not anxious to get back in case
John turned up.

But the viscount was already in the
parlour when they returned, talking
animatedly with Aunt Sophie.

'Oh, dear me!' Felicity heard Aunt
Sophie exclaim as she and Aunt Jane
took off their bonnets and pelisses in
the hall.

What news had he brought that had
excited Aunt Sophie?

On entering the parlour, Felicity
was relieved to see both the visitor
and Aunt Sophie were in the best of
spirits.

John's eyes on her made Felicity's
heart flutter, and although already rosy-
cheeked from the exercise and fresh air,
a deeper blush coloured her cheeks.

'Do tell us what's amusing you,
sister,' Aunt Jane cried after polite
bows were exchanged.

'I don't know where to start!' Aunt
Sophie raised her hands to her flustered

face as her agitated steps took her back and forth.

'May I explain?' John smiled at the ladies.

'Please do, sir,' Felicity said eagerly in her voice he loved to hear.

The viscount gave his full attention to Felicity. He noted her graceful figure, her presentable although not fashionable clothes; the lively expression on her bespectacled face. Yes, he thought her a most agreeable lady. Indeed, she was the kind of woman who would suffice for what he had in mind.

'I have discovered your maid gave your necklace to the man, Jake, you mentioned,' he said to her. 'The fellow tried to sell the jewels in London, but was unable to. So he sailed for Amsterdam early this morning.'

'Amsterdam?' Aunt Jane echoed, eyes wide.

'Indeed, ma'am. Amsterdam has a thriving jewel market.'

'Oh, dear!' Aunt Jane exclaimed.

'Now you will never get your lovely necklace back, Felicity.'

Aunt Sophie stepped forward and put her arm around Felicity's shoulders.

'Don't give up hope, my dear. His lordship has a plan.'

'Hmm!' John said, with a smile on his lips. 'I discussed this with Miss Ward before you came in. I suggested you three ladies might like to accompany me on a visit to Holland.'

They were too polite to gasp but John heard the trio draw in their breath before he continued.

'You might spot your maid — or recognise the necklace — if we all go and seek them there.' His eyes flashed. 'Besides, I have some business to do in Amsterdam, and would be grateful for your company. I will of course pay all your expenses.'

Felicity almost screamed with joy. A trip abroad, how delightful!

'Amsterdam is where my uncle Jan lives,' she said. 'I should love to meet him.'

John watched her eyes dancing behind her glasses. It made her seem beautiful.

'Your aunt told me you have Dutch relatives,' he said. 'We will, of course, endeavour to visit them.'

'Why, yes, my uncle is a jewel merchant. He may be able to help us find my necklace.'

John, Viscount Coombe, charmed by her enthusiasm for his scheme, bowed.

'So I understand.'

Felicity thought he had done well to set them on pursuit of her jewels. But he seemed to be a trifle too competent in the way he was organising them all to go to the Netherlands so quickly. Her dear old aunts, although not fools, were trusting. She, however, suspected . . .

'And may I ask what business you are to undertake in Amsterdam?' she asked.

'Government business,' he answered smoothly.

Before she could question him further,

Aunt Sophie chipped in, 'And his lordship proposes that we sail the day after tomorrow — so little time for us to prepare!'

Aunt Sophie had already decided to take up Viscount Coombe's generous offer, and said so. Aunt Jane agreed with her sister as she always did.

'Then, why don't you go and start your packing?' Felicity suggested. 'I will beg his lordship to stay a few more minutes, as I should like to ask him a question.'

John bowed. In their excitement her aunts couldn't get out of the parlour door quickly enough.

'Your lordship.' Felicity's expression became serious.

'John, if you please.'

'Very well, John. I must admit I always think of you as John, because of us not knowing your title at first.'

'As I think of you as Felicity — the bringer of happiness. Anyway, there are just too many Miss Wards for me to deal with!'

Felicity smiled. She did like him, and trusted him — up to a point. She said, 'I must ask you what government business you are engaged in.'

'You are an astute young lady.'

'No longer young, sir.'

'Young enough.'

She looked at him sharply. He seemed as though his tongue had raced ahead. What was she young enough for?

'Hmm,' he said immediately to cover his slip.

'Stop humming with me, sir. You seem to make a habit of concealing the truth!'

Surprised at her directness, he looked at her with faint amusement that annoyed her.

She directed her glasses severely at him as she continued, 'You have been most kind to track down what happened to my necklace, and I thank you for it. But this sudden departure for Amsterdam makes me wonder. I know my dear aunts are overjoyed at the prospect of the trip, as indeed I am. Nevertheless, sir . . . '

'You are quite right, ma'am. You have every right to question me. Now . . . '

Felicity stood attentively watching a man she knew to be intelligent and competent, yet at that moment appearing somewhat at a loss for words.

'Perhaps it would help you to know that my father knew your father, Earl Wanstead,' she interrupted. 'And that we know they both thought highly of each other. My aunts also made enquiries about your character . . . and we feel we can trust you.'

John beamed, his steady gaze making her feel suddenly weak at the knees.

'I'm glad to hear I pass muster. You and your aunts need have no qualms about my intention to protect you during this trip.'

'Then please tell me what I am not aware of,' she said, suddenly cross. 'I should like to know why you are so anxious to help me find my necklace?

Why indeed a titled gentleman bothers to concern himself with us elderly ladies? And what is this mysterious government business you are engaged in, pray?'

'I counted three questions, ma'am. Which one would you like me to answer first?'

'You are being flippant, sir!' Now she was angry!

The viscount's smile vanished.

'Very well, I will confess, only it might take a little while. Shall we sit down?'

His hand waved to a chair and she sat obediently before he drew up a chair close to her. He gazed at her and she did not lower her eyes.

'First of all, Felicity, I will assure you that I happen to like you and your aunts. I really would appreciate your company in Amsterdam. And I shall make every effort to find your stolen property, and locate your mama's family, too.'

Felicity gave him a weak smile.

'Very well, I believe that much. But what of the cost of taking the three of us, plus my aunts' maid?'

'I am well-off.'

'And we are not. You are also an aristocrat and we are only lesser gentry. Don't you think our lack of fashionable dress will show you up?'

'I have considered that.'

'I expect you have. You weigh up everything.'

John's mouth lifted at the sides.

'And so do you, ma'am. I know I shall hide nothing from you so I do not intend to deceive you, or your aunts. Your respectability is perfect.'

'And exactly what is your business abroad, sir?'

A flush came to her face as he edged his chair nearer so that accidentally their knees touched. His voice became deeper and confidential.

'As I'm asking you to trust me, then I shall trust you to keep the information I am about to impart a secret too. Felicity . . . I've been

41

asked to take government bonds to Amsterdam. Money is needed from Dutch merchants for an army to fight Napoleon.'

'But Bonaparte is a prisoner on Elba!'

'He was. He escaped last month.'

John's large warm hand enveloped hers.

'Don't concern yourself. There will be no danger to you or to your aunts. Napoleon is in the south of France gathering an army. We'll be back in London before he reaches Paris!

'Wellington is going to Brussels to prepare his defences. The action is taking place far from Amsterdam.'

'Then why should the Dutch care?'

'The Dutch are anxious to prevent the French from occupying their land again, and are willing to lend us money to buy provisions for the army to fight him.'

Felicity looked searchingly into his calm eyes. She felt sure he was telling the truth. But talk of war on the continent was disturbing.

'Are you sure there is no danger?'

'Well,' he continued quietly, 'the bonds I carry are useless to anyone if they are stolen. Someone of repute must carry them if they are to be honoured. Of course, if the French knew I had them, they might want to prevent me from arriving at the bank in Amsterdam . . .

'That is why I have been asked to deliver them unobtrusively. You and your aunts will give me cover. There, ma'am, now you have it all. Now, you must tell me if you think I am expecting too much to ask you to accompany me?'

The tip of her tongue flicked around her lips. She still had the feeling he hadn't told her everything!

But she longed to have the trip abroad; to meet her mother's family; to have the chance to recover her necklace.

Nor did she wish to disappoint her aunts who were thrilled at the prospect of visiting Amsterdam.

'I think,' she said dismissing her qualms, 'we shall go.'

'Bravo! I admire your spirit very much, ma'am.'

Felicity felt she was prepared for any adventure, but she quelled her mounting sense of excitement and said firmly, 'Promise me no harm will come to my aunts.'

'I do. And will you promise me not to tell anyone what you know of my business?'

'It's a bargain.'

Their eyes met and held as though sealing a pact. As they both had much to do before leaving the country, his lordship left immediately.

When he'd gone, Felicity felt happy as she had discovered the truth. But tripping upstairs to pack, she remembered she'd not asked him why he was showing particular friendliness towards her.

She was certain there was something else in his mind he had not revealed.

Perhaps something he wanted her to do?

She hoped it was nothing important, as she decided to try and forget her unease. When the time was right she would question him further. Until she knew exactly what his lordship was planning, she could not help remaining slightly perturbed.

But in the meantime all her thoughts had to be directed towards collecting her modest belongings — without the help of her maid — ready to leave for Holland.

★ ★ ★

The male servant accompanying Viscount Coombe on his trip abroad looked burly — and sharp — Felicity thought when she saw him. He wore no livery, but like his master was neatly and simply dressed. This made Felicity feel content that her, and her aunts' attire, was in keeping with his lordship's appearance.

But she knew why it was he did not want to outshine them. He had to appear as an ordinary gentleman travelling with his two aunts. She herself would pass as his sister — anyway, that was how she chose to see it.

The hired carriage drew up at their Kensington house, and he hopped out to greet the ladies and helped them into the carriage.

He called to his servant, 'Tom, collect the ladies luggage if you please and lift it on to the coach.'

'Yes, sir,' the servant answered with a grin, and promptly did as he was told.

That strong-looking manservant will be a useful member of the party, Felicity thought, comforted to think that they would be well protected.

They were soon on their way and Felicity could relax knowing his lordship would arrange everything perfectly for them.

'I do believe your smile has not left your face since I came to fetch you, Felicity,' the viscount commented, looking at her in amusement as the carriage neared the docks.

'It's the prospect of going abroad,' she assured him with shining eyes, thrilled to see ahead a landscape of ships' rigging. 'Ladies seldom have adventures.'

'I hope we do not have an adventure!' he murmured. 'A carefree trip is what I want for us all.'

'Oh, but an adventure would be fun!' she retorted.

4

Although Aunt Sophie and Aunt Jane were not good sailors and Felicity spent some time helping their maid to comfort them, it did not prevent her from enjoying the experience of sailing over the Channel.

'You are most attentive to your aunts,' Viscount Coombe commented approvingly as she took a turn with him in the fresh breeze on deck.

'They have always been most kind to me,' she assured him with her bright smile that always made him smile back.

'How are the ladies feeling now?'

'Queasy, I fear. But I'm sure they'll recover quickly once they are back on land.'

'Which should be soon, the captain tells me. The wind has been in our favour. Look over there, you can just see a strip of land.'

His arm had slipped around her shoulders as he directed her to where he was pointing.

It was a brotherly gesture she did not take amiss, but his nearness and the thrill of feeling his firm hand on her back sent a delightful shiver down her spine.

'I can't see anything but a dark line on the horizon.'

'Don't you remember your geography lessons?' He chuckled. 'The Netherlands are flat. Dykes, canals and windmills are what you'll see.'

'Not in Amsterdam.'

'Indeed. From the old centre of Amsterdam there's a ring of concentric canals with broad quays on either side, making the city's plan moonshaped. The Herengracht, the Keizersgracht, and the Prinsengracht are cut by a pattern of radial streets.'

'You didn't tell me you knew Amsterdam!' She regarded him severely. 'As usual, sir, you are keeping something under your hat!'

'No. I'm merely trying to give you a picture of Amsterdam, ma'am. But as you are about to see it for yourself you'll find my words could not do its beauty justice.'

She moved a strand of hair which the wind had blown across her face.

'It may be that I find Amsterdam as charming as you say. But I repeat, sir, I'm constantly surprised to find out what you do not tell me!'

His eyes looked down searchingly into hers.

'And I repeat that I do not intend to deceive you, Felicity. I think too highly of you. Perhaps it is because I'm unused to women's company that I don't satisfy a female's endless curiosity.' His grey eyes narrowed as he looked thoughtful, pressing his lips together. 'I see I have not convinced you. Perhaps you have some further questions to ask about me about my motives? Ask away, I'll endeavour to answer them all, and I promise to be honest with you.'

Struck dumb by his sincerity she

considered the questions she would love to ask him. Such as, what he really thought of her . . . and if he had any other close lady friends — but she dare not ask. Felicity merely smiled faintly back at him.

'No questions? Don't tell me I've cured your curiosity already?' he said teasingly. His head had lowered, his face was very near hers, and it seemed as though he had in mind to kiss her — and she would not have minded one bit!

With a sharp intake of breath she turned her head away to hide her reddening cheeks. Her heart raced. Was this first exhilarating trip abroad making her lose her commonsense?

His lordship had merely stooped to speak in her ear because this lively wind would have blown away his words.

What a silly goose she was allowing her imagination to run away with her. Why on earth would handsome Viscount Coombe want to kiss a plain old maid?

In Amsterdam the wide canals and the characteristic brick houses that lined them enchanted the ladies. New sights and smells thrilled Felicity, whose enthusiasm had her leaning out of the carriage to look at everything, much to his lordship's amusement.

'My goodness that must be the fifth windmill I've seen already!' she exclaimed. 'And just look at the different gable ends of those houses against the sky.

'How strange it is to see the Dutch men in their baggy trousers and clogs and the women's strange head-dresses.' Her eyes sparkled as she turned to speak to him. 'Holland is most impressive!'

The viscount felt an inner warmth to have pleased Felicity so much, and was thankful that so far his mission was without mishap.

The inn he selected for their stay was orderly and clean. The viscount spoke a little Dutch, and had soon organised the servants to take their luggage up to the three rooms he had generously allowed for them.

To her delight, Felicity found her room looked out over the canal. She could watch the activities of the people on the tree-lined streets on either side of it.

With the busy canal craft passing by her window, too, she had constant entertainment.

Unlike her aunts who were tired after the journey and wanted a meal and their bed, Felicity was alive with eagerness to see the city.

'You are not eating your meal, Felicity. Are you not well?' Aunt Jane scolded, who had quite forgotten her ill health on board and was happily attacking her supper.

'I'm too excited to eat, Aunt.'

Felicity was not sure if her lack of appetite was due to the strange-tasting food, the thrill of being in Amsterdam — or some other unsettling feeling in the pit of her stomach that she could not quite place, but made her feel exhilarated — especially when she was close to John.

She looked at him eating quietly by her side. His thoughts appeared to be far away. What was he thinking, she wondered.

'Are you venturing out tonight, my lord?' she asked.

Off guard, he swallowed, and quickly took a sip from his wine glass.

'Well, I thought I might take a stroll.'

'I wish I were a man and could come with you,' she said wistfully.

'I'm glad you are not!' he retorted.

Felicity looked sidewards at him in mock surprise.

'Why? I should have thought you might like a companion to visit a drinking house this evening.'

'Felicity, really!' Aunt Sophie protested. 'How can you say such things!'

His lordship grinned.

'My dear aunts, please do not concern yourselves.' He turned to her and said silkily, 'Felicity and I have a pact to be open with each other, have we not?' He put a gentle hand on hers.

Felicity for some reason was very conscious of his hand and although she didn't exactly object to it, she blushed. It made her feel very feminine.

'It is becoming overcast already, Felicity,' Aunt Sophie scolded. 'You'll have plenty of time to look for your relatives and explore the city tomorrow.'

So Felicity had to be content with going to bed early. She felt herself fortunate, however, as she could gaze down from her chamber window at the scene below.

Dusk came and the darkening streets were lit by the lamplighter. But she did not light a candle, preferring to sit in the increasing darkness and observe the panorama outside.

The view was magical. The street lights made the dark water on the canal gleam, and patterns formed on the water as barges slid by. To her right there was a bridge spanning the canal, so that she could watch people with carts, mothers with little children and men returning tired after their day's work hurrying home.

After an hour or so the cobbled streets became almost deserted, and only the occasional sounds of the many street sellers, dogs barking, men guffawing and the merry cry of a woman's voice broke the evening's stillness.

Felicity thought of John, strolling alone in Amsterdam. She would have loved to be with him. He was not too top-lofty to find a jolly bar and enjoy the company of drinking men.

She hoped he had taken Tom with him and would be safe. Until he had delivered the government's bonds, he might be in danger. Perhaps that was why he was so thoughtful at suppertime. It was a pity they had arrived so late he could not deliver them until morning.

She must have dozed, but awoke to

find herself still sitting by the window and she shivered as the night air was cold. Outside the scene had changed very little, only there were far fewer craft on the canal, and even fewer people about.

The tinkling sound of a distance clock chiming made Felicity realise it was, to her amazement, midnight. She must go to bed, be well rested for seeing the sights in the morning.

Drawing the curtains before lighting her candle, a sudden movement below caught her eye.

Holding the drape which had not yet been fully closed, she was fascinated to observe a dark figure dart over the canal bridge. Then another as if chasing him.

She saw the first man racing along the street as if making towards the inn.

But yet another man had appeared, as if to cut him off, and he headed for the dark shadow of a tree. The little drama held Felicity spellbound.

Two men appeared to be chasing one. A gleam of metal made her blink. Had one a pistol in his hand?

She clutched the curtain. No, surely she was not watching a crime about to take place!

For a minute they remained still like chess pieces: no-one moved. Then she saw the first man was indeed moving. He was edging towards the inn again.

She gave a low cry. It was John!

He was trying to get to the inn and was being prevented from getting to the door. The man stalking him — with the gun — was probably intending to shoot him!

Horrified, Felicity breathed in great gasps! With her hand on her heaving bosom she blinked down at the fraught situation. In a flash it occurred to her that John must be saved for his important mission. She needed him. Nay, she loved him!

She must slip downstairs and open the inn door, which would be surely locked at this time of the night, and allow him to run in quickly without hammering for the landlord to open up.

Without concern for her own safety, Felicity grabbed the candle. Her hand shook in her haste to light it.

Swiftly leaving her chamber she hurried along the passage and down the steep steps towards the front door.

Indeed, it was locked and barred. Putting the candle down on the flagstones, she began to unbolt and with great effort to push up the bar, which was heavy for her to remove.

She was panting with the effort of removing the heavy bar, and wiped the sweat from her brow before rushing back to turn the knob — but the big oak door was locked!

Trying not to panic, she swung around and looked for the key. Where would the landlord keep it?

She picked up the candle again and began to search. Her heart was almost pounding out of her chest. She looked up and saw there was a big key hanging on a hook.

It must be the door key. But she could not reach it. She stood on tiptoe. Still she was not high enough to lift it off the hook. She jumped and tried again, and again. But with no success.

Desperate, she looked around for something to stand on. Fearing what might be happening outside while she was struggling to open the door she found herself sobbing with anguish.

The furniture around was big and heavy. She told herself firmly that if she was to help John, then she must keep calm. There must be something somewhere to stand on and help her reach the key. Then she saw a kitchen stool.

Placing it beside the front door, she clambered on it to reach the key. In her haste, she fumbled as she tried to push it into the keyhole, but at last it went in and with a loud squeal the key turned.

She pulled at the heavy door, edging

it open and looked out. The street lights were all she could see outside. All was so quiet.

Eventually her eyes became accustomed to the dark shapes of the trees and the gleaming canal water which had small waves in the wind. But nothing else moved. Blinking back tears she tried to find the voice in her dry throat.

'John,' she called softly. 'John, are you there?'

There was no response. Had he been caught? Or shot while she was scrambling for the key?

Felicity opened the door wider to take a more careful look at where she last saw him. Was it the swirl of a cloak she saw?

She knew it was recklessly unsafe for her to stand here with the inn door open wide.

It was certainly unseemly for a woman to stand like this in the doorway but it was John's safety she was thinking of.

A dark shadow of a man suddenly

raced towards her and she felt sharp needles of fright all over her body. A gun fired and the figure fell.

Felicity realised with a flash of fear, the shot man must be John.

Wanting to run to his aid, her commonsense told her not to. What use would she be to him if she were shot, too?

'John, crawl nearer and I will help you,' she called in a loud whisper.

Her heart hammered as she saw him raise himself and pull his injured body towards the inn entrance.

Further shots sounded around her and the sight of him crawling painfully towards her became too much. Without considering her own safety, Felicity picked up her skirt and flew to assist him, half dragging him to safety as a bullet whistled by them.

At last inside the inn, Felicity fell to her knees to examine the bleeding wound on his leg.

'Lock the door,' Viscount Coombe gasped.

As Felicity rose and began to push the door closed, a man's racing footsteps could be heard approaching. Her heart pounded as angry shouting filled her ears and she threw her weight behind the heavy door. But the man behind it was far stronger, and she was no match for his strength and had to yield.

His large booted foot prevented her from shutting it, and soon the great bulk of his dark form was easing himself in.

'Let me in, ma'am,' an English voice cried. It was Tom!

By this time, Felicity could see very little as her glasses had fallen and smashed on the stone floor. Confusion swept over her as the entrance seemed to be crowded with men, and a loud babble of Dutch and English was being spoken.

She heard a bang as the heavy door was shut and the key being turned, followed by the sound of the locks being shot home. The bar was being replaced by a man she realised was the landlord, when, to get out of their way, Felicity walked backwards and tripped over the stool. She fell, bumping her head on the hard flags.

5

Waking to the sound of women's voices, Felicity felt for her glasses which she usually kept by her bed. Then she remembered she was not at home, and it had been the adventure of last night which had caused them to break.

She rose on one elbow to blink at the blurred figures in her bedchamber. The plump figure was unmistakably Aunt Jane, and she recognised Aunt Sophie's voice, too. The other figure was taller.

'Aunt Sophie,' she called feebly, 'how is John . . . I mean, his lordship?'

'Ah, my dear. So you have woken up at last,' Aunt Sophie cried.

The three figures loomed nearer her bed.

'I would feel more comfortable if I could see you better, Aunt. Unfortunately, I broke my glasses last night.'

'I know, my dear. We will get you some more. Now, the doctor would like to know if you are in pain.'

Felicity lay back on her pillow.

'A slight headache and a few bruises, that is all. I only had a tumble, Aunt Sophie.'

'It was a nasty fall, my dear.'

'I'm sure I'm almost recovered. Now please tell me how is his lordship?'

'We understand he is sleeping late, too. I suspect he had a little too much Dutch beer last night!'

Felicity realised her aunts knew nothing of the viscount's mission, and the subsequent attempt to kill him.

Longing to know how his injury was, she nevertheless knew it was wiser to keep her mouth closed.

'Perhaps I can visit him later,' she muttered.

'Go into a gentleman's bedchamber! Indeed you can't. I just don't know what's come over you recently, Felicity. You seem to be living in a world of your own. Quite lacking in propriety!'

'Yes, Aunt,' Felicity said submissively but with a little quirk on her lips.

Of course her aunt was right, she should not even think of going to see John in his bedchamber.

But somehow she just could not think of him as an ordinary gentleman; she had treated him for some time as though he were a close friend.

She decided she would ask his servant how he was. The doctor having seen his patient conscious and talking in a lively manner, excused himself and left the room. Struck by the thought that she did not know what her aunts had been told of her accident, she enquired, 'I have little recollection of how I fell . . . '

'Down those dreadfully steep stairs,' Aunt Jane obliged. 'I must say I don't like going down them myself.'

Aunt Sophie joined in.

'And it was most fortunate that the innkeeper heard you fall, and fetched his lordship's servant, Tom, to carry you upstairs to bed.'

So her aunts had been told a reasonable story to explain what had happened to her last night. Felicity sighed with relief as she lay back on her pillows.

Then she sat up again sharply. She thought of how she had chided John for keeping the truth from her. She was no better!

But it was sensible to leave her aunts thinking nothing sinister had happened last night.

She would go along with the idea they had that his lordship had come back drunk, and she had fallen down the stairs. Any truthful explanations would only upset them.

Feeling satisfied that their injuries were explained, and had not upset her aunts too much, she said, 'I'll get up presently. I'm looking forward to seeing Amsterdam.'

'Indeed you will not! You will stay where you are. Anyway, you won't see much until you have some new glasses!' Aunt Sophie declared.

Felicity didn't argue.

Without eyeglasses she wouldn't see well. In fact, she was quite glad to rest in bed while her breakfast was brought up to her.

By the time she'd finished her meal, she was chafing to get up but felt she must oblige her aunts and rest.

As the afternoon became sunny, she was permitted to sit outside for a short spell in the inn's courtyard garden, which was colourful with exquisite tulips and sweet-smelling hyacinths.

She asked a maid to fetch Tom, and looked around to make sure no-one was about before she whispered, 'How is his lordship?'

'The doctor attended him, and in a few days he will be well enough to join you,' Tom assured her.

She looked up at Tom's honest face and felt she wanted to pass a message sending her love to the stricken viscount, but thought it might sound too forward.

'Please take him my best wishes

for his recovery,' she said formally, confident that no-one knew of her feelings for him.

The following day, a visit to an optician was their first venture out. As Felicity walked along by the canals she felt frustrated as she could not see much. She hoped she would be able to see all the interesting sights a little better when she got her new glasses.

'I must say I'm surprised by Viscount Coombe's lax behaviour,' Aunt Sophie declared as they walked toward the shops. 'I wouldn't have thought that he was the sort of man who would become so inebriated he would have to be confined to his room for a long period!'

Felicity longed to explain why it was John was abed. She took a furtive glance at Tom who was accompanying them. The loyal servant did not attempt to contradict the ladies' opinion of him either.

'He is probably suffering from an exceedingly sore head — and serve him right!' Aunt Jane said, puffing as they climbed over a canal bridge. 'But he's been his usual caring self to direct us to a reputable optician so that Felicity can acquire a new pair of glasses. And has generously provided us with ample florins for our shopping expedition.'

Felicity knew John to be a kind, caring man; a brave one, too. Her heart went out to him as she knew he must be feeling very frustrated having to stay put on his sickbed when he had the government bonds to deliver.

She hung back a little to speak privately to Tom, whom, she noted, did not appear to be other than his cheerful self.

'Do you think it is wise for you to leave his lordship unprotected, Tom?'

'The landlord has found a good man to tend him, ma'am.'

'But, the danger . . . '

'There's no danger now, ma'am.'

Felicity glared at him. Did Tom know about the bonds? She dare not mention them, or say more, as she had to hurry to catch up with her aunts before they noticed her lagging behind.

The Dutch maker of glass and crystal lenses was a skilled craftsman. Felicity tried several lenses to assist her sight.

The glasses she obtained eventually were far better than the old ones she had broken, and the new frames more attractive on her, so she was delighted.

After doing some shopping, the ladies were happy but quite exhausted when they returned to the inn, with Tom carrying their purchases. They saw a smart carriage was parked outside the inn, and before they had reached the door, a distinguished-looking gentleman emerged.

He bowed to the ladies before climbing into the carriage and the equipage moved away.

'Who was that?' Aunt Sophie asked.

'His Excellency the British Ambassador, ma'am,' Tom answered promptly, 'visiting his lordship.'

'Well, you surprise me, Tom. I should have thought Viscount Coombe would want to keep as quiet as possible in his present disgraceful condition.'

Felicity smarted at the jibe, but thought quickly and suggested, 'Perhaps the Ambassador is an old school friend of John's and is paying him a visit?'

Her aunts did not challenge this suggestion, and continued to their rooms intending to refresh themselves before dinner.

Felicity's face burned with embarrassment of having to mislead her dear aunts again, but considered it was better for them that they knew nothing of John's importance to the government.

Guilt struck her as she remembered that John himself believed in deception for a good cause. She had been too hard on him, and longed to see him again to make amends.

★ ★ ★

When Viscount Coombe appeared at the door of their private parlour after breakfast two days later, his face appeared to radiate happiness as he approached them.

He looked splendidly well, apart from a stick he used to assist his wounded leg.

'So you hurt yourself in your drunken state, did you?' Aunt Jane said scornfully, but her smiling eyes showed she was not really being too severe on the handsome, young man.

'Ma'am, I regret my evening out did end in somewhat of a disaster,' he confessed with a bow, but turned to give Felicity a brief smile.

'Well, I hope you learned your lesson, sir, and there'll be no more inebriation!' Aunt Sophie declared. 'Anyway, we have to thank you for the florins you kindly sent us. We have enjoyed our days in Amsterdam very much. And Felicity is most grateful to you for her new glasses, aren't you, dear?'

Felicity's colour rose as his keen grey eyes were directed on her. He seemed to want to say something to her, but he just smiled. Finding her voice, Felicity said, 'Indeed, yes. They are excellent glasses. I thank you most sincerely for them, sir.' She gave him a quick curtsey.

'I'm very pleased to hear it, ma'am. I would say, yes indeed, I think they enhance you,' he assured her after examining her flushed face intently.

Then he gave her a quick smile and a polite inclination of the head as if he truly meant it.

Felicity bloomed under the sunshine of his approval. But her aunts were as pleased to see him as she was, and gave him all their attention, bade him sit with them for a while, giving Felicity no chance to have a private talk with him.

Felicity had to be content with seeing him almost fully recovered. Having him in good spirits was a pleasure for her.

She could gaze admiringly at him from afar; observing him far more clearly than she used to.

Not only could she perceive his wide

shoulders under a well-tailored, navy jacket, and cream trousers covering his long, straight legs, but also his keen grey eyes, his noble nose . . . and his lips she yearned to kiss. With the strength of her ardour she amazed herself! What a disgraceful way for a maiden lady to think! Then she reminded herself that he was a strong character, too — a man who kept secrets.

'I have some news of your family, Felicity.' John made her start as he broke into her thoughts as he turned suddenly to beam at her. 'Your uncle, Mijnheer Mander, has been traced, and he wishes to meet you. He has asked us all to visit him.'

So although recovering from being shot and confined to bed, he had not wasted his time in Amsterdam.

Most probably he had asked the Ambassador to get one of his staff to find her Uncle Jan. Viscount Coombe was not an army officer, but he was certainly a commanding gentleman!

'Thank you,' she said, feeling strangely unable to say anything else as she fought the urge to throw her arms around his neck and hug him.

She did not like to ask him if he had also made any progress with finding her necklace.

But knowing he always kept something up his sleeve she raised her head to gaze into his twinkling eyes, and felt sure he would not have forgotten about that quest either.

'Well,' Aunt Sophie said, looking pleased, 'I think we are able to pay Uncle Jan a visit today.'

'Oh, good.' Aunt Jane clapped her hands together.

The Viscount gave a laugh.

'There, Felicity, your aunts are keen to meet him as soon as possible, as I'm sure you are. Shall we organise the hire of a carriage so that we may go today?'

Felicity felt a strange mixture of keenness to see her uncle, and yet apprehension.

What if her Uncle Jan was as cold

and unsympathetic as her brother? She would feel so embarrassed.

But on reflection, she felt sure Viscount Coombe could manage any man, even her unkind brother, Augustus.

Then she remembered the bonds. She said quickly, 'I would, of course, like to find my family, but I was thinking, sir, that perhaps you have another important task to undertake first.' She mouthed the words: 'You have government bonds to deliver.'

She was annoyed when his lordship stared back at her impassively. He seemed to be planning something else. Meanwhile, her aunts looked at each other with puzzled expressions.

'Don't talk in riddles, Felicity. His lordship is quite capable of making his own arrangements. You do not have to remind him of what he should or should not be doing!'

'Of course, Aunt. It is just that as this is the first time he has felt well enough to go out, I thought he may wish to do something else.'

'Really, Felicity! You are incorrigible!'

John just stood there smiling, as though he had no idea either what she was talking about.

But she knew he was intelligent enough to understand perfectly what she was hinting at. Well, she had done her best. The government bonds were his responsibility, not hers. She prayed he would get them to the bank tomorrow.

Piqued and feeling a little foolish, Felicity glared at him. Although she was smitten by his charm, Viscount Coombe's mysterious behaviour could infuriate her at times!

The Viscount said to them, 'I will send a message to say we will visit before noon. And order a coach for five o'clock, if that will suit you ladies?'

Her aunts squealed their delight and said they would go and prepare for the outing.

'Will that be convenient for you, Felicity?'

'It will,' she snapped, curtseying.

'Excuse me, I must sit and rest my leg,' he said, looking as though he might collapse as he looked around for a seat.

Felicity's attitude changed. The poor man was still suffering from his leg wound. His face looked strained with pain. Without hesitation she leaned over to take his arm and assist him over to the settle, and rang for a servant to bring him a drink.

Aunt Sophie and Aunt Jane rushed over to fuss over him for a few minutes, but finding him better for taking his weight off his leg, announced that they would leave him in Felicity's capable hands.

He seemed to recover very rapidly when they had the room to themselves and the maid brought in a pot of coffee. It was a ruse. The wretched man had deceived her aunts again — just so that he could speak to her alone!

'Will you pour?' he asked her.

She did, saying in a hushed voice,

'Why did you pretend not to understand what I was saying about the bonds?'

He caught her hand, calming her agitation. Looking up into her cross face, he said gravely, 'My dear Felicity. The bonds have already been safely delivered. I went out that first evening for a private meeting with bank officials. It was just unfortunate that a French spy had been tailing me, and shot at me on the way back to the inn. As Tom dispatched him, I'm no longer in any danger.'

'Oh!' she gasped. There was no knowing what this aristocrat, John, Viscount Coombe, might do or say next!

He squeezed her hand, sending a delightful warmth through her body. He added confidentially, 'You saved my life, Felicity. You have my deepest gratitude.'

'Nonsense!' she said, slipping her hand out of his grasp. 'It is I, and my aunts, who have so much to thank you for!'

'In that case, we are even.'

She nodded and smiled.

'That's better. I like to see you smile, Felicity. It is like your name — it brings sunshine into my life.'

'Then you had better give me reason to smile,' she replied, not intending to agree that she would allow him to get away with any more deception.

'I don't know that I am capable of always coming up to your high expectations, ma'am.'

She laughed merrily.

He sat back basking in the enjoyment he was deriving from her company. She was no beauty, but for him she possessed many attractive features: her lively, straightforward and mature disposition appealed to him; he judged her as a kindly woman. Those glasses did not spoil her brown, intelligent eyes and long, curling lashes.

Her shiny, dark brown hair was nicely arranged. She had a slender, gently curved figure which would be the envy of many women of her age.

And her contralto voice had taken his fancy from the time he'd first met her.

Most of all, he felt he was right in thinking she was the woman he could quite happily spend the rest of his life with.

When she sat down gracefully opposite him, he smiled knowingly at her. Felicity was quick to notice. Now what plan had he got in mind, she wondered.

6

Felicity heard the rain and turned to look at the heavy droplets on the diamond-paned window. John guessed her thoughts, saying, 'Don't let the weather worry you. We have some work to do.'

'We?' Felicity echoed, sitting straight-backed in anticipation.

'Well, I have someone, and something, to find,' he said with a smile on his face, 'and knowing how competent you were assisting me in my last mission, I would appreciate your help before you go and see your uncle today.'

Felicity was suspicious, but couldn't help being fascinated by the mischievous look in his eyes, which was not entirely disguised by his diplomatic mask.

She leaned forward and whispered, half-jokingly, 'Not another adventure, my lord?'

He paused, studying her face seriously. Then said, 'I should hope not!' before breaking into a grin and making her believe the opposite.

Felicity hadn't entirely enjoyed her last adventure, but the call to perform some bold action again nevertheless intrigued her. She had the same need to be challenged as she sensed he had.

With Viscount Coombe, she told herself, she would always be safe. She would miss his company terribly when she went back to England, therefore she would take the opportunity to be with him now.

'What is it you want me to do?'

'Tom has discovered where he thinks your stolen necklace may be. My present state has not allowed me to pursue the lead until today. It would help me if you would come and identify your necklace.'

'Why, my lord, I can't see any danger in that!'

'Tom tells me the man who may have it is no gentleman.'

When John moved a little closer so that they could talk in hushed voices, she felt awash with the pleasure of being so near him. It was all she could do not to touch the hair framing his face and press her lips on his.

The agony of being in love with this lord who was so near her, yet knowing he would not be interested in a plain old maid like herself, made her face flame scarlet.

He ignored her blushes as he continued softly, 'I understand that your necklace — if indeed it is the same, and only you can tell me that — may well be up for sale this morning, at an inn not far from here. The robber, Jake, also may be their trying to dispose of the gems.'

'It seems an odd place to sell them.'

'Dutch merchants traditionally held bulb auctions at inns. Even today private transactions frequently take place in taverns, both legal, and illegal. Innkeepers encourage sales, as it provides them with good profits as the traders sometimes stay overnight and eat and drink heartily.'

'And which female will dare accompany me into this den of thieves?' Felicity questioned.

'I thought you might go with your servant, Bet, who has been found.'

'Bet has been found? But, sir, she should be in gaol. That girl stole my precious necklace!'

'Indeed. And she's very sorry now — about the theft. Tom found her starving on the streets, and had no difficulty in persuading her to admit to what had happened. The man, Jake, was merely using her, as he must do other maids, to steal from their mistresses. He makes the poor creatures think that he loves them, only to take the valuables and leave them as beggars in some foreign city.'

'How wicked! He should be caught before he treats anyone else the same way.'

'I agree with you. As for Bet, although many would have her hanged for theft, I think she has some virtue in her.

'Therefore, I have in mind to send the girl back to England so that she can be placed in honest employment.

'It will prevent her from falling into a life of crime if she stays here with no means of support. She is still very young, and was foolish. Now I believe she has been taught a lesson and should be given a second chance.'

Felicity's anger with her maid disappeared.

'That's most noble of you, my lord. Bet, I recall, was from an orphanage, and the lure of marriage, and easy money, must have been hard for her to resist. She is not the only one who has deceived others, I think.'

He stared at her thoughtfully.

She took a slow breath.

'Well, I'm prepared to take her back, John, if my aunts agree. And, I think they are more likely to agree if my necklace is found first.'

'That is most kind of you, Felicity.'

When Felicity was taken to see the bedraggled maid cowering to keep warm by the inn kitchen range, she was sure the poor girl had indeed been punished for her wrong doing.

'I'm sorry, miss, I'm truly, truly sorry,' was all Bet could mutter, over and over again.

'I accept your apology, Bet. There is no need for you to say you are sorry any more.'

Bet stopped crying and looking up gratefully, promising that in future she would be trustworthy.

Felicity glanced at Lord Coombe who nodded, and she loved him all the more for his goodness in suggesting Bet could be given a second chance.

'Very good,' Felicity said briskly. 'Now, Bet, we need your help to recover my necklace. So get up quickly as I want you to come with Lord Coombe and myself to find this man, Jake, who has harmed you as well as me.'

The maid was on her feet in a trice, eager to please.

'First, I will find you a warm cloak, then we'll go.'

The changed girl looked adoringly at her mistress, making Felicity feel glad the girl would be protected from further evil. They were on their way within the hour.

Lord Coombe had advised Felicity to wear a drab, hooded cloak, and wrap up warmly.

So she sat in the coach with her hands warm in a muff. Her heart sang to be with the man she adored by her side.

Tom, and two strong men, who, his lordship explained, were Dutch constables, accompanied them on horseback as they rode off to the inn which was some way out of Amsterdam. The weather had not improved by the time they were surrounded by the flat Netherland countryside, which appeared grey with rain.

A vicious wind sent the women's

cloaks flying as they dismounted from the coach in a small village.

The inn, when they entered it, was crowded.

'They're doing brisk business,' Tom commented to his master.

'Ah, but what kind of business?' his lordship returned drily.

Although protected by the menfolk, the prospect of having to search the inn, noisy with men's guttural shouts and laughter, made Felicity hesitate.

'I'm ever so scared,' Felicity heard Bet say through her chattering teeth.

'Come along, Lord Coombe will look after us,' she said stoutly, taking the maid's hand and following in his lordship's footsteps with the two constables following close behind them.

'Look for Jake,' Lord Coombe had to shout to the maid over the racket.

It was difficult for the women to move around with men's bodies filling the drinking rooms. There were many rooms in the inn, many deals being made, and much contention as well as good humour with the loud bargaining.

Felicity's head began to ache with the effort of easing herself, and her maid, through the congested building. As she was pushed and knocked, she longed to ask John to remove them from the noisy place.

But looking up at his grim determination, and knowing his injured leg would not be spared in the scuffle, she held her tongue.

She would be patient, and endure, until she was certain Bet had seen every man in the inn. They were here after all for her benefit, looking for her jewellery. Having searched the downstairs they managed to push their way upstairs.

'That's Jake!' Bet said suddenly, pointing to a young man with a sharp face, extravagantly dressed, and seated at a table opposite another man with whom he was discussing business.

Jake's eyes observed he was being watched. Scooping up something which gleamed into his pocket, he glanced nervously around. Noticing Bet with the constables, he quickly reached inside his jacket and drew out a pistol.

Bet screamed. The man with Jake slid away and suddenly they were all in danger of being shot.

'Put that gun down, man!'

His lordship immediately limped forward, and showing no sign of fear grasped Jake's wrist, to force him to release the weapon.

Felicity's heart hammered as she watched the men struggle, and Viscount Coombe yelled over Jake's curses at the two Dutch constables to come quickly and arrest the villain.

Jake was soon overpowered and hoisted to his feet. But with a cry of rage he lashed out at the constables, freeing himself from their grasp, and slithering away through the crowds before they could manacle him.

The fleeting glimpse of evil on Jake's face made Felicity shudder as he darted off. Then she felt John's firm arm around her, supporting her, and rested her head against his broad chest hearing his heart beating after exertion.

'He's got away,' she said distraught.

'I doubt it. Tom's downstairs.'

And when the women were escorted outside, they found Jake pinned to the ground by Tom.

The constables took over and secured their prisoner more effectively. They searched Jake and held up the jewels he had in his pocket up for Felicity to see.

'Yes, that is my necklace.'

'You'll never prove it!' Jake crowed before the constables led him away.

'We'll see about that!' his lordship said, handing the necklace to Felicity who put it into her reticule.

Back in the carriage, Felicity found herself still shaking, but his lordship's arms came protectively around her. His body soon warmed her and stopping her from shivering.

Bet was overjoyed.

'There, milady, Jake's going to get what he deserves.'

'Dutch liqueur, my lord.' Tom said, appearing with a tray of small glasses. 'Recommended to put the life back into you.'

'What will they do with Jake?' Felicity said, taking a sip of the burning liquid.

John drained his glass and smiled appreciatively as he returned his empty glass to the tray.

'He will be kept in custody, until his trial.'

Felicity turned slightly and looked up at his face inquiringly.

'It has occurred to me it might be, as he said, difficult to prove the necklace is mine.'

'That is our next task, to prove that it is yours,' John said, smiling down at her.

'Do you have an idea how you will do that?'

'Indeed I do.'

Felicity lay back on the carriage swabs and sighed. Yes, of course he would have some ideas. It both amused and amazed her to think that he was always one step ahead of her.

But she did love and trust John, Viscount Coombe. He had shown himself to be courageous, capable, and ingenious and the British government had trusted him with their bonds. And she felt no qualms in her mind now, that although he liked to keep his plans hidden, he could be relied on.

Also, she reasoned, it was intriguing being with a man who continually made interesting revelations.

However, she did wonder what else he'd got stored up there in that devious head of his!

★ ★ ★

They had lunch as soon as they returned to Amsterdam, and as Aunt Sophie and Aunt Jane were full of chatter about visiting her Uncle Jan, there was no need for Felicity to mention her morning's adventure.

However, the viscount, who had

become increasingly friendly with her aunts, surprised Felicity by telling them a little about their morning outing.

'So you have recovered your necklace, Felicity!' Aunt Sophie exclaimed delightedly. 'That is indeed good news.'

'And the thief has been captured.'

Aunt Jane smiled and clapped her hands in approval.

'Bet has been found, too,' the viscount added.

'Bet?' the aunts questioned in unison.

'My maid,' Felicity said.

'Where is she?' Aunt Sophie inquired, after a silence.

'Here. And she tells me that she regrets stealing from me, and her foolishness of having being taken in by a rogue.'

Felicity looked at her aunts and noticed neither was anxious to condemn the young girl. She then turned to the viscount who was clearly waiting for her to speak.

'His lordship and I think she has shown true remorse, and should be given another opportunity to live an honest life.'

Felicity waited for her aunts' decision.

'Well,' Aunt Sophie said slowly, 'if you both think we can now trust the girl, then I have no objection to having her in the house again.'

'Nor I,' Aunt Jane chirped.

The ladies beamed at each another. For some reason the viscount began to laugh. Felicity turned on him.

'What amuses you, my lord?'

'You've made me very happy.' His attention was on her as he gave her a broad smile. 'You are as a lady should be; brave, kind and forgiving.'

'My lord, I think it is you who have those fine qualities,' she said quietly.

On impulse he leaned towards her and gave her a gentle kiss on her cheek, which sent Felicity's blood racing and she felt herself heated in confusion.

Not daring to look up at him, she turned away and began to pick at the hem of her dress.

Felicity was aware of the turmoil she

felt. Yes, she was pleased now he had told her aunts what they had done that morning. She was glad to find he was honest, although his methods of going about things was sometimes unusual.

But she still felt very anxious, longing to be able to show her love for him. The problem was, she knew her love was doomed. A wealthy and important aristocrat would never marry a plain woman like herself.

Their objectives for coming to Holland were now almost over. The sooner they returned to England, and parted, the better. She would just have to learn to live with the heartache of not having the man she so desperately wanted.

7

When Felicity arrived at her uncle's house in the old part of Amsterdam, she could see at once that it had been built for a prosperous merchant.

Its reflection, a fine sandstone façade with Corinthian pilasters and garlands between the windows, gleamed in the canal water in front of it.

Adjusting her spectacles and patting her hair in place she murmured, 'Oh, dear, my best gown is not going to look very fashionable for this grand-looking place!'

'You always look elegant to me,' John said in all seriousness.

'It is sweet of you to say so,' she replied, not believing he really did find her agreeable.

She didn't realise that her graceful and slender figure in her simple gown, and her sparkling blue eyes behind her spectacles, made her look adorable to him.

Felicity noticed her aunts nod and exchange secret smiles, and felt irritated. If they thought John was courting her, it only added to her burden of knowing their love was never to flourish and bring her happiness. A feeling of apprehension struck Felicity as she entered the grand house to meet her Uncle Jan for the first time.

When he came to greet her she found he had some features that reminded her of her dear mama.

Bitter-sweet thoughts flooded her mind. Her happy childhood came back to her, and reminded her of the pain she'd suffered not only from the death of her loving parents, but her subsequent loss of means and status owing to the meanness of her brother.

Uncle Jan knew a little English, just as John knew a little of the Dutch language.

After greeting each other, they were

shown upstairs into the drawing room where a great many people of all ages were gathered.

'They are members of your Dutch family,' John whispered in her ear.

She was touched as the ladies and gentleman, and children, stepped forward to kiss her, smiling as they greeted her in Dutch.

'Uncle Jan,' she said turning to look up at the tall Dutchman, 'please thank them for their hospitality, and say that I'm delighted to meet my mama's family.'

'And we, too, are very happy to see Agatha's daughter,' he said haltingly in English after he had delivered her message.

He had such a kindly face and a twinkle in his blue eyes, she felt he spoke the truth.

Felicity's apprehension soon disappeared. Her lack of knowledge of their language in no way spoiled the pleasure of being received warmly by the family, although she became somewhat alarmed when they seemed to regard Viscount Coombe as her prospective husband.

She was placed next to John at the table, and although he had a fair understanding of Dutch and turned to her many times to translate some of the merry conversation for her, she felt embarrassed that she could not explain to the party that they were only friends.

After dinner the viscount asked Felicity to show her uncle her necklace, which she did.

'Ah, yes, yes,' Jan nodded after examining it.

He bowed and left the room returning later with a jewel case which he opened to reveal two beautiful sapphire earrings, and the place where a necklace and a brooch had once laid with them.

'See if your necklace belongs here,' Jan said.

Felicity carefully put her necklace in the place designed for a necklet, by the earrings, and cried, 'Why it fits perfectly!'

'There is your proof of ownership, Felicity,' his lordship whispered.

Her uncle beamed and closed the box then handed it to Felicity.

'These jewels belonged to your grandmother, Agatha. She gave the necklace and brooch to your mother when she went to England to marry your father. She kept the earrings for herself so that she had something to link herself with her daughter living abroad. A lovely gesture, don't you think?'

'Why yes, indeed it was,' Felicity agreed. 'Where the brooch is now I do not know. But as a little girl I remember Mama wearing the necklace, and I have always loved it.'

Viscount Coombe explained how it had been stolen and how they had managed to find it. Jan closed the lid of the jewel box and addressed the family in Dutch.

Felicity thought he was telling them about the theft. Her uncle turned to her and bowed as he handed her the box.

'Now that your grandmother is dead, we think they should be yours, Felicity.'

Everyone showed their approval of the gift, and Felicity accepted it graciously.

Felicity enjoyed the evening so much she felt like her Aunt Sophie and Aunt Jane, reluctant to leave the family party when it was over.

'I wish you happiness,' Jan told her as he bid his niece goodbye. 'I was worried about you when I heard your brother had taken your mama's fortune, and left you with nothing.

'But I see your aunts care for you, and Viscount Coombe loves you and will make you a fine husband. Our family wishes you every happiness in the future, dear Felicity.'

Flabbergasted, Felicity flushed scarlet. She dare not look at John who was close by.

She just hoped he had not overheard her uncle's sentiments. On the way back to the inn he was politely attentive to all three ladies.

In the remaining days of their trip abroad the viscount seemed anxious to please them all. He escorted them to various places of interest and tulips bloomed everywhere. His leg wound had healed, and it seemed to Felicity that he was entirely content. She only wished she wasn't suffering from constant heartache.

* * *

Their business and sightseeing in Amsterdam complete, it was now time for them to return to England.

Rumblings of war were being felt on the continent, and although the social life in Brussels was thriving, many cautious English people were returning home.

Viscount Coombe prepared his party to get away safely before the hostilities with Napoleon began.

Felicity hated the thought of being

separated from John. Steeling herself to the necessity of having to eventually part from him she tried to detach herself from her romantic feelings.

But it was not easy for her to pretend she did not love the viscount. She ended up by trying to avoid him.

'Is there something wrong?' he asked her, when at last he found her alone on the deck of the ship when they were sailing back to England.

'Oh, no, thank you. I'm just a little sad to be going home.'

'So, you enjoyed your visit?'

She gave a little laugh.

'Very much thank you — except for some dangerous moments!'

'You are not as keen on adventures as you thought then, Felicity?'

'It depends on the adventure, I think. Ours were a little hair-raising, although necessary.'

'And successful. The bonds are delivered and Jake is caught.'

'Yes, indeed.'

They both gazed out at sea for a

while. They did not talk, each deep in a reverie as light sea spray showered over them. It was John who broke their silence.

He inched closer to where she was standing, his eyes intently watching her viewing the swell and fall of the waves.

'Will you marry me, Felicity?' he said suddenly.

For a moment his words did not sink into her mind. For a while she continued staring at the horizon, thinking she must be dreaming.

'I'm not sure I heard you correctly.'

'I asked you to be my wife.'

She glared back at him, thinking he must be teasing.

'What scheme have you in mind now, pray?'

His dark eyebrows knotted as he ran his figures through his damp hair. Now that he had found the lady he wanted to marry, he hadn't expected she would be reluctant. He would never understand women!

He stood looking down at her disbelieving expression.

'But I am asking you, Felicity.'

His deep voice and grey eyes were bewitching. It would be so easy for her to simply say that she would be honoured.

She inhaled a deep breath of salty air. Why was she hesitating when the man she loved was asking her to marry him? It must be because she felt he couldn't be serious.

It was as if she was sure he must have another reason, or a plan of some sort, but he would not say what it was.

He hadn't said he loved her. He merely thought she would be suitable. But what for? Had he perhaps a beautiful mistress he loved hidden away and he wanted her to fulfil the rôle of his wife on the surface, for the sake of respectability?

'I won't agree to marry you unless you tell me exactly what your reasoning is.'

Viscount Coombe stared at her. He

had never expected a marriage proposal could lead to this tangle.

'Felicity, you are a sensible girl, you must see that I need a wife. I am already thirty five years old, and my father — '

'Ah, so your father wants you to marry!'

'Of course he does. He wants me to have an heir. Is there anything wrong with that?'

Bright spots stained Felicity's cheeks and she turned away from him. Kicking her toe against the side of the bulwarks her eyes looked out to sea as she asked, 'So you think I will suffice?'

His lordship cleared his throat.

'Indeed, you will do very well.'

Felicity sensed he was embarrassed, too. He had admitted the truth, she was sure of that, but did she want a marriage of convenience?

Yet, despite any schemes he might harbour, she knew deep down that she loved him.

She wanted to stay beside him

always, and agreeing to a marriage of convenience would enable her to do that. She didn't think he intended to be unkind and she felt sure he would always treat her with respect. So, although he did not love her, the match could bring some happiness to them both.

'Well,' she said, 'if you think I'm suitable for your requirements, I have no objections to being your wife.'

He gave her a gentle kiss.

'Good,' he said beaming down at her.

He looked pleased with himself which only made her feel more frustrated to think he might be keeping something from her.

'John, might you change your mind?'

'Good heavens, Felicity, no! Are you sure you want to do me the honour of marrying me?'

'I am.'

He gave her a wonderful smile that sent her briefly into heaven. But her face fell again when she recollected he was only offering her marriage — not love.

Seeing her doubtful expression he added, 'I believe we will cope well together, but if you wish, we can delay announcing our betrothal until you feel absolutely sure about it.'

'I . . . '

'I understand. You were taken unawares by my sudden proposal. I thought we were well in tune with each other. Now I realise I should have chosen a better time to ask for your hand. Forgive me.'

'Oh, John, there is nothing to forgive.'

'Then you wish to think about it. I will leave you now to your own thoughts.'

He took her hand and kissed the inside of her wrist which sent a thrill through her body, before bowing politely.

Watching him walk away, her heart was thudding with emotion. How she longed to run after him and put her arms around him, and beg him to tell her he loved her.

But he was obviously not a passionate man. Her plain looks would not inspire any passion in him for her anyway.

And if she wanted to marry him she would have to accept him the way he was.

She reasoned that of course, there were many unscrupulous women who would wed him solely for his title and his wealth, but she genuinely loved him, and would always care for him if she became his wife.

Taking a quavering deep breath she decided.

Yes, she would tell him, and everyone, that she would be very happy to be Lady Coombe.

'My dearest Felicity,' Aunt Sophie said after she was told the news, when they were back on land, 'I'm absolutely delighted that you and dear John are to marry.'

'We always said there was a romance brewing between the two of you,' Aunt

Jane said with a wide smile on her face.

Felicity wished with a pang of regret that there was a romance ahead for her, but smiled at her aunts.

They intended to enjoy her wedding as if she were their own daughter, and Felicity did not want to spoil their pleasure by giving any hint of her reservation about the coming event.

'Dear aunts, you have both been so kind to me,' she said. 'I will miss you. I trust you will often come to stay with me?'

'Indeed we will, Felicity,' Aunt Jane said excitedly. 'As well as a town house, his lordship has a house and estate near Stamford, he tells us. So we will be travelling up and down the great North Road to see you whenever the weather allows.'

Fortunately, his lordship was fond of her aunts and liked the idea of seeing them.

John seemed in the best of spirits since Felicity agreed to marry him, and readily agreed to anything she suggested or wanted. His kindness was almost painful for her . . . if only he would understand her need to be told she was loved.

8

They were all tired after the long sea crossing, and having hired a coach at the port, Tom piled their luggage on to it, while his lordship assisted the ladies to step inside.

'Much as I enjoyed our trip abroad, I'm glad to be back in England again,' Aunt Sophie said.

'I'm looking forward to getting home and having some tea,' her sister exclaimed.

John had his thoughts on something a bit stronger. And looking across at his betrothed, he considered a brandy might chase away his uneasiness about what was upsetting Felicity.

Now that she was betrothed to him, she should be looking happier. Deep in his heart he felt quite sure they were well suited, and that she liked and cared for him as much as he did for her.

She was perhaps wary, thinking he held a trick up his sleeve when he asked her to marry him, which he didn't, and he would have to try and convince her of that as soon as he had the opportunity.

His concern soon shifted to a more immediate problem. As the carriage started moving and they began passing through the docklands towards the city, they hadn't been travelling more than a mile when their coach stopped. He could see that they were in a built-up area of tumble-down houses.

There was obviously some sort of hold-up on the narrowest part of the road ahead.

A queue of impatient traffic had built up. Drivers shouted; horses reared and neighed; many passengers stuck their heads out of the carriage windows yelling to know what was delaying their journeys.

'What have we stopped for, Tom?' his lordship called out to his servant who was riding aloft.

'There's been a carriage accident, sir.'

His lordship sprang out of the carriage and strode ahead to see for himself. He came back to report to the ladies.

'I'm afraid the stage coach ahead has broken down. Completely blocked the road. It seems impossible to pass it for a while, and as there are other carriages piled up behind us, we are boxed in.'

'Travelling these days is abominable,' Aunt Sophie grumbled. 'Now I suppose we won't get home till after midnight!'

'I'm so thirsty,' Aunt Jane wailed.

Tom's face appeared at the carriage door.

'Your lordship, I've been told the stage horses in front have broken loose and run off with the fore-wheels. Men are needed to catch them. Shall I give them help?'

'Very well, Tom. I'll escort the ladies to the inn over there and obtain some refreshment for them.'

'Oh, that is most kind of you!' Aunt Jane twittered.

Alighting from the coach John looked around at the rundown houses and remarked, 'This area is not the best. I hope we will not be delayed for long.'

His fears were increased when he became aware that there must be a garrison stationed nearby; the place was full of red-coated soldiers.

John was not very happy. The inn was confoundedly busy, and he didn't like the crowds.

He would have left the ladies in the coach if he'd realised, but he'd already promised them coffee and he had to get them one.

Felicity and her two aunts, accompanied by the two maids, were ushered by his lordship into the inn where a hot and bothered landlord and two serving wenches were trying their best to serve the raucous soldiers together with other passengers from the delayed carriages.

No private parlours were available, but a group of officers, seeing the ladies, offered the party their table.

'That is most civil of you,' Aunt Jane declared, sitting herself down and smiling up at their boyish faces and dandyish uniforms.

'Our pleasure, ma'am,' the oldest of the group said, a Guards captain, magnificently attired in scarlet and gold lace. And by his weather-beaten looks, he was a Peninsular veteran.

The soldiers seemed in no hurry to leave and stood around the table talking to the party.

'So you are off to fight Napoleon Bonaparte again, are you?' Aunt Sophie inquired.

'Indeed we are, ma'am. On the next tide we'll be off. And we'll need the luck of the devil.'

Aunt Sophie smiled up at him.

'I admire your bravery, fighting for your King and country.'

Aunt Jane agreed.

'I admire all men who will risk their

lives to fight and protect us from his ravages!'

'Not all men like to dirty their hands,' the Captain remarked pointedly looking across at the non-uniformed viscount.

John stared back coldly at the toughened soldier. If the ladies were not present he would have been happy to teach that jackanapes a lesson. As it was, he knew he was odd man out, surrounded by the camaraderie of uniformed men.

Only Felicity knew he had already done his country a service. But she, too, was slightly at odds with him. It was best for him to ignore the insult so as not to cause trouble.

'Hmm. I'll try and find a server to bring us some drinks,' he said.

'Good man,' the captain called cheekily, turning his empty wine bottle upside down. 'How about filling the fighting men's glasses up, too?'

The other young officers quickly swilled the rest of their wine so that they had empty glasses, too, then grinned hopefully at his lordship.

Being treated like a servant, to fetch and carry, and expected to pay for the soldiers' as well as his own party's drinks, was almost more than John could stomach. It took him all his self-control to prevent himself from flaying the lot of them.

It was no easy task persuading the busy landlord to serve him when so many people there wanted their beer tankards filled, but eventually his lordship managed to obtain a tray of coffees for the ladies, and a couple of bottles of wine.

When he returned to his party, he found the ladies laughing and enjoying being entertained by the officers, which he decided was no bad thing as it made the ladies enforced wait more tolerable, for them at any rate.

But he observed, too, what Felicity seemed not to have noticed, that the captain's eyes were not on her aunts, but fixedly on her.

Already made irritable by the inconvenience of their delay, and the heavy presence of so many soldiers, his lordship's temper was further provoked on seeing his love being blatantly observed by the cocky Guards captain.

When their glasses were refilled, the officers rudely ignored his lordship, but John was pleased to see the ladies continued to laugh and chatter with the group of officers.

Shrugging his broad shoulders, he decided to leave the party for a few minutes, and made his way out of the inn to see how the situation fared outside. The road was still blocked.

Like hornets, the angry crowd of delayed passengers was buzzing with anger; iron-shod hooves clattered on the cobblestones as the restless carriage horses shuffled in their harnesses and pawed the ground. They were all impatient to continue with their journeys.

His lordship went to their coach.

'Any sign of my man?' he asked the coach driver.

'He be just a'coming, sir,' the coachman replied, pointing with his whip.

His lordship squeezed his way through the crowd and hailed Tom.

'Is all well now, Tom?'

'Just about, sir. The coach that crashed has had one wheel repaired, and its stage horses found and are not harmed — they only took fright. When they're calmed down a bit, the coach will be on its way and this jam should ease.'

'Very good. Come, let's collect our party, and be ready to move on.'

When the two men entered the inn and eased their way towards the ladies' table, John was struck dumb. Felicity was missing. And so was the captain.

'Where's Felicity?' he barked.

The merry party's eyes turned towards him. His fierce expression wiped the smiles from their faces.

'She was here a moment ago,' Aunt Jane piped up.

'Yes, but where is she now?' his

lordship demanded.

Everyone looked around, and even the officers reacted as though John were a senior officer and stood smartly to attention.

The crowded room was promptly searched, but the two were not to be found.

'Tom, escort the ladies to their coach immediately, if you please. I will look for Miss Felicity.'

To Tom he whispered, 'Take the ladies to their home if I do not return with Miss Felicity before the traffic has cleared.'

'Aye, sir.'

Tom immediately set about his task, and with the assistance of the young officers, they helped the aunts to their feet and escorted them through the crowded inn and back to their carriage.

His lordship breathed deeply. At least he felt he could trust Tom to get them home safely. A sudden pluck on his sleeve made him look down to see Bet's anxious face.

'I'm sorry I didn't see Miss Felicity leave, sir. Let me come with you and help find her.'

Rubbing his chin, his lordship knew he had to decide whether he could trust the maid to be discreet when Felicity was found. He felt sure now his love had been spirited away by the captain.

'Yes, come. Miss Felicity will need a female companion.'

He collared the young officers before they slipped away and asked them to help, too. They obliged, not daring to disobey the viscount, who displayed a more commanding air than they had at first realised he had when they were baiting him.

They began by making a thorough search of the crowded inn. They questioned some customers, the landlord and the serving wenches. They went into the inn kitchen to speak to the cook, and looked upstairs. But although the inn was full of people no-one had noticed the captain or the lady leave.

When no trace of them was reported,

his lordship knew he would have to look farther afield. Knowing the Port of London district from his past forays, he started to organise a wider search.

He fought to keep a cool head, when his mind kept picturing the captain's lewd glances at Felicity.

Felicity, he knew, was no green girl. But his lordship knew her to be wellbred; carefully nurtured; always protected by her aunts, and quite unprepared for the advances of a tough soldier.

Also Felicity was his love now. He loved her, and felt increasingly worried about her safety.

Deploying the young officers to hunt in the buildings surrounding the inn, he took Bet with him along the street to where he remembered a derelict wharf nearby.

The Thames in this area contained large amounts of sewage and the odour was foul. No wonder the former residents had fled the houses to avoid the pestilence.

Bet did not complain but trotted along beside the viscount like a faithful hound. Something sparkled on the ground. A surge of love for her overcame him as John bent down to pick up Felicity's spectacles.

'We are on the right track, Bet,' he said grimly.

They stopped every now and again to step into a deserted building, but only disturbed a rat or two which then raced off.

'Listen!' His lordship laid his hand on the maid's shoulder.

'Sir, there's someone over in them sheds I reckon,' Bet said darting off so that his lordship had to take to his toes and run after her.

The nearer they came to the old workshop, the unmistakable sounds of human voices became clearer. Before he even saw her, John recognised Felicity's cries.

★ ★ ★

Felicity had not been aware of the captain's devilry until too late. When her aunts were engaged in a lively conversation with the young officers, she, too, was enjoying the lively exchange of humorous anecdotes.

When the captain whispered in her ear that there was a lady injured in the coach crash, needing the comfort of another woman, her response was to go and assist.

When Felicity realised that the injured lady was not at the inn, she said to the captain, 'I ought to tell my aunts that I am leaving to tend this sick person.'

'There's no need, ma'am,' the lying captain said. 'I have told one of my junior officers,' and taking her arm tightly he propelled her through the back door of the inn.

Although Felicity disliked being manhandled, she didn't suspect she was being abducted. In the stable yard, there were horses, carriages and ostlers about, and it was only after they had walked over towards the gate that Felicity asked, 'How much farther, sir?'

'Just down this street.'

Felicity frowned, feeling something amiss.

'I can't go alone. You must know . . . '

Of course he did! She suddenly realised she'd been duped. Like a thoughtless schoolgirl she'd fallen for his ploy to remove her from her companions.

'Let go of me, sir,' she said, suddenly angry, trying unsuccessfully to remove his large hand gripping her sleeve. The captain's face showed he was oblivious to her dismay.

'Sir, if you do not return me to my aunts immediately, you will have to answer for this extraordinary behaviour.'

'To whom?' he crowed.

'My betrothed, Viscount Coombe.'

His laugh was unpleasant.

'So that man with you is an aristocrat, is he? A coward, unwilling to stir himself to fight.'

'His lordship has done more for his country than you could ever do!'

Ignoring her protests, he continued to shove her down a street and into a deserted alleyway.

Undignified though it was, Felicity did her best to try to release herself. But with no success.

Her cries for help became louder as she realised her peril, but the brutish captain had dragged her away so quickly they were now far from anyone who might hear her.

'You are hurting my arm!'

'You'll be released soon, my pretty,' he jibed.

Felicity tried to think as her heart pounded in fright. His lordship will find us, if only I keep my head and allow him time. With her free hand she deliberately removed her glasses and dropped them so that they slid down the folds in her skirt, hoping the captain would not notice. He did not.

Delay him, she thought, trying as far as her strength allowed to try to slip from his grasp time and time again. But in the end he picked her up and slung her, sack-like over his shoulder. Without her glasses and the daylight fading, Felicity could hardly see where she was being taken — to some waste land where the stench made her retch.

On reaching a dilapidated, wooden building he tossed her inside. Pain hit her, her body jarred by the tumble on the hard floor. With his feet apart he stood over her and she felt numb with fear.

'Now you are mine!' she heard him boast.

The captain appeared to her as only a blur, which was as well as his brazen expression and depraved behaviour would only have upset her all the more as she was struggling to get up.

'You dare touch me further and . . . I'll scream,' she cried helplessly.

'Don't waste your breath, ma'am. There's no-one around here except me to hear you.'

She heard his heavy breathing; felt his hard kisses and his groping hands. Her piercing cries begged him to stop. Voices outside made the captain straighten to alertness.

Running footsteps were followed by Lord Coombe's bellow, 'Come outside, you blackguard!'

Felicity was suddenly aware of Bet's arms around her.

'Oh, miss, we was terribly worried about you.'

Men's groans, and the sound of knuckles landing on hard bone and flesh could be heard outside.

'His lordship,' Felicity gasped, 'is in danger . . . that brute of a captain is a seasoned soldier.'

Bet left her for a moment or two then came back to comfort Felicity.

'Don't you worry about his lordship, miss. It's that captain who's getting the worst of it.'

Moments later, painfully easing his coat over his bruised body and torn linen shirt, his lordship came in and kneeled by Felicity. His big hand enveloped hers.

'Are you able to walk?'

Blinking through her tears, Felicity gulped, 'Yes, I've not been hurt.'

'Thank God,' he whispered as he tenderly replaced her spectacles.

Remorse hit her on seeing he'd been beaten; her voice trembled as she tried to explain.

'I was brought here against my will. It was very stupid of me to have believed the captain . . . he told me someone was injured.' She gave a shudder. 'They needed my help, he told me.'

He gently squeezed her hand.

'We must get you back to your aunts' house. It has become darker so no one will notice the state we are in. We should find a carriage for hire at the port.'

With the viscount supporting her shivering body, and Bet on the other side of her, she tried to regain her composure as they walked away from the noisy place. And with the viscount's knowledge of the area he soon located the cabs for hire.

All the time, Felicity was aware that she'd behaved like a fool. She'd stupidly allowed herself to be compromised. What upset her more than anything was that she felt herself besmirched.

As they were not officially betrothed, the viscount may not now want her as his bride. Her mind was racked with the thought she had that day both gained, then lost, the man she loved so much.

In the carriage, John cradled her in his arms, and spoke only the softest words of comfort, seeming only anxious to get her home as quickly as possible. Just as the carriage reached the aunts' front door, his lordship bent his head to whisper to Felicity and she saw in the lamplight the kindness in his eyes.

'May I advise you to say nothing of your ordeal, Felicity. You are in no danger now, and it's best forgotten.'

He then turned to her maid.

'Bet, you are to hold your tongue

about this evening's events. You must never even hint at what happened, or say that your mistress was ever out of your sight.'

'Sir,' Bet said earnestly, 'you have my word on it. You was both ever so kind to me and I'll never forget that. I promise you I never heard nor saw nothing improper this evening.'

'Very good, I shall trust you to keep your word, Bet.'

'Now, Felicity, please convey my good wishes to your aunts when you go in. I shall not wait to speak to them, as I am in no fit state. My tattered and bloodied appearance will only cause them distress. It may take several days for my black eye to repair, so I will visit then.'

Although her voice was cracked with emotion she managed to murmur weakly, 'Thank you for coming to help me, my lord.'

While the coachman rang the doorbell he helped her step out of the coach.

'Good-night, my dearest Felicity,' he

said, bowing and kissing her formally on the hand. 'Do not allow yourself to dwell on this unpleasant episode. It is over, and must be forgotten.'

Before the front door bell was answered, his lordship had left the two women standing on the doorstep, and disappeared back into the coach which promptly moved off.

9

Felicity, are you out of sorts?' Aunt Sophie enquired a few days later as they were finishing their breakfast. 'You've hardly had anything to eat this morning.'

Felicity came back from her day-dream.

'I am very well, thank you.'

But Aunt Sophie persisted.

'It seems to Jane and I that you are bearing up under some strain, instead of relishing your coming marriage.'

Her aunts, refreshed after their trip abroad, had began the preparations for her wedding with gusto.

'I sometimes can't help wondering,' Aunt Sophie continued, 'if you really want to marry Lord Coombe.' She looked at her niece fixedly. 'Well?'

Felicity gave an embarrassed, little laugh.

'Why, of course I do!'

'Then what ails you?'

'Nothing. I've told you, I am quite well.'

Both aunts stared at her, then turned to look at each other. Aunt Sophie shook her head slowly.

'She is not very happy, I can tell.'

Aunt Jane gave Felicity a sympathetic smile, then said to her sister, 'Perhaps that's how one is when one is in love, Sophie.' She gave a long sigh. 'Not being married ourselves, perhaps we don't know what it is like to be in love.'

'Fiddlesticks!' Aunt Sophie retorted.

Felicity looked at her aunts, wondering if indeed they had ever been in love, and knew the agony and ecstasy of it.

'His lordship certainly seems to be avoiding coming to see you. When did he say he'd visit again?' Aunt Sophie asked.

'If you remember, I explained that he said he was going to be excessively busy for a week or so.' She repeated the excuse she'd given them: 'He told me as he'd been away for at least a few weeks, he had a great deal of estate work to oversee. But he intends to come and see us as soon as he is able to.'

She forced herself to eat a little breakfast. The fib she told was probably true, although she did wonder as she ate breakfast how long black eyes took to heal.

Aunt Sophie poured herself out another cup of coffee saying, 'Very well, but in the meantime do us the kindness of showing at least a little enthusiasm for your coming nuptials.'

Felicity forced herself to smile at her two good-natured aunts, trying to hide her qualms which were causing butterflies in her stomach.

She'd been told by Aunt Sophie that she'd been given a generous allowance by his lordship for a new wardrobe.

She was well aware that most women would be thrilled to have an opportunity to clothe themselves afresh.

And as her marriage was to be a marriage of convenience, Felicity did not see anything amiss in accepting his lordship's kind gift. And she most certainly needed to improve her clothes before she appeared in Society. Only her heart wasn't in the task.

Felicity's aunts had never moved in the highest circles of society and knew little of what was fashionable. Fortunately, her maid was interested in fashion, and turned out to have surprisingly good dress sense.

Not only was Bet enthusiastic to assist her mistress, but seemed to know what would suit Felicity.

The girl had been taught to sew well at the orphanage, too, so her help with the make up of the fabrics was invaluable.

Occupied with shopping, garment making, and other wedding preparations, Felicity's time was filled, but her thoughts frequently strayed to thinking about John.

How she longed to know what he

truly thought of her. He was so adept at hiding his thoughts and plans.

She wondered endlessly if he had any deep regard for her, especially now after the unfortunate escapade at the docks. It hadn't been her fault, although she'd witlessly acted like an idiot and fallen for that evil captain's wiles.

But after breakfast on that bright May morning, she decided her aunts were right: she shouldn't be downcast. She was to be married to the only man she would ever want.

True, she'd been abducted — but nothing had happened. She had not been ruined in the eyes of Society because they would never know about it. John had immediately forgiven any foolishness on her part, and instructed her to forget the episode.

Her maid, Bet, was proving to be a treasure: completely trustworthy now; most willing to serve her.

Felicity was very pleased with her and she was so glad she'd decided to take the girl back after her wrong-doing.

Contentment began to flow through Felicity; she realised that she really had no need to succumb to any more self-torture. Therefore, she was in the best of spirits when Lord Coombe called to see her later that day.

Dressed in one of her new morning gowns made of a pretty floral muslin which enhanced her slender figure, she whirled in front of her cheval glass and decided she looked quite passable for a plain woman of twenty-seven. Bet had skilfully coiled up her dark hair and only wisps of curls framed her face. She felt for the first time in her life quite elegant.

To John, she looked as graceful as a nymph entering the parlour and curtseying to him.

'Felicity, you look adorable!' he said in amazement, even before bowing.

He strode over to take her hand to raise it to his lips. Looking into her beautiful dark eyes — which shone just as brilliant as her necklace — he returned her welcoming smile. Then taking advantage of the privacy of the parlour, he kissed her lips instead.

Set afire by his show of passion, Felicity glowed. She did not mind that he did not seem to want to release her hand, and remained looking up into his peaceful, dove-like eyes for some time. She thought it heavenly to be so near him, and found she could unashamedly look up at his handsome features for ever.

At last she said, 'I fear you'll have those marks on your face for ever, always reminding you of my stupidity.'

He squeezed her hand.

'Hush, Felicity. We said we would talk no more about that incident! I, too, have done things in my life I would prefer to overlook.'

'You're very kind.'

'Do you forget that I'm indebted to you — most of all because you've brought me happiness?'

Felicity knew she should be able to

say that he had brought her happiness, too. And partly he had. She felt she couldn't say that so instead she said, 'I must thank you for my new gowns.'

His smile widened as he stepped back and looked at her from the top of her glossy hair to the points of her kid slippers.

'If your gowns are all as charming as the one you are wearing, then it is I who will receive the pleasure of seeing you wear them.'

Why was it, she wondered, that he seemed willing to praise her, but he would not say that he loved her.

'I'm happy to know that I shall do you credit.'

She smiled, thinking his tailor certainly knew how to make the best of his fine male figure, and now, by giving her a new wardrobe, he had made sure that she would look quite adequate by his side.

'Felicity, before our betrothal is placed in The Times, I should like you to meet my father. Do you feel ready to meet him?'

'Ready? Why of course. My gowns are almost finished, if that's what you mean.'

'Not exactly.'

'Then explain.' Oh, dear, what was he concealing from her now?

'Let's be seated.'

He fetched her a chair, then one for himself. He flicked his coat-tails back before being seated a little nearer to her than a gentleman normally would, so she eased herself away from him.

'No, don't sit far away. I don't want to have to shout at you across the room.'

She smiled and obediently moved herself back where she'd been so close that their knees were all but touching, thinking she would dispense with proprietary; she loved being close to him.

His lordship beamed before his face became serious. He cleared his throat.

'My father lost his wife many years ago. He is not familiar with . . . I mean, he is not used to the company of women.'

'Do you mean he has not replaced his wife, nor has a close female friend?'

'Precisely so. He does not seem to like female company.'

'Yet he told you that you should marry.'

'Yes, he did. But I don't dislike females.'

Felicity blinked.

'And because, I believe you said, he'd like you to have an heir?'

'Precisely so.'

Felicity looked down at her clasped hands and wriggled her fingers. She took a deep breath, then looked up and said, 'Of course I'd be delighted to meet your papa. If he's short-tempered with me, I'll understand.

'And as we are travelling north, I think we should also pay your brother a visit,' John replied.

'Should we?'

'He is the head of your family.'

Felicity sighed out loud.

'I'm afraid I must tell you that Augustus and his wife don't care for me. They think I'm far too plain to be associated with them.'

John's wide smile broke into a chuckle.

'I'm sure when they see you now they'll get a surprise.'

'I'm sure when they see you, they certainly will!' Felicity laughed in reply.

Yes, it would be amusing to see the expression on Augustus's face when he learned his spinster sister was to marry a handsome, wealthy viscount!

Although Felicity was not particularly looking forward to either visit, knowing that both John and her aunts were to accompany her made the prospect seem more tolerable.

Lord Wanstead lived near Huntingdon, and as Felicity's brother lived in Hertfordshire, it was decided to call on him first.

'We think your brother Augustus has treated you shamefully,' Aunt Sophie said to Felicity, as they were picking flowers in the garden to take round to a friend who was ill.

'We only need spend a little time with him,' Felicity said, plucking and smelling a sweet-scented rose. 'Besides, I'd like to see my nephews and niece. Beatrice and Augustus have three children now.'

'Well, I just hope Augustus does not prevent you from marrying Lord Coombe.'

'How could he do that?' Felicity cried.

'Augustus was crafty enough to take your inheritance!'

Aunt Sophie snipped a few more stems.

'Felicity, much as I like and admire your intended, I'm not sure he could stand up to a pompous bully like Augustus.'

Felicity merely smiled as she put the flowers she held carefully into the trug hanging over her arm.

'That, my dear aunt, remains to be seen.'

'Well, I won't appreciate seeing John

being . . . er, browbeaten.'

'Neither would I!' Felicity retorted. 'But rest assured it won't happen!'

For the first time, Felicity felt she was going to enjoy meeting her brother again.

Aunt Sophie looked at her sharply.

'I feel that there is definitely something odd going on. I do not know what to make of your behaviour. Earlier this week you were acting as though you were reluctant to marry his lordship. Now you are defending this man as though he is your hero!'

'Oh, but he is!' she declared. And not wanting to pursue the matter in case her aunt asked probing questions about her declaration that his lordship was heroic, she looked around for some distraction. 'Oh, dear, I think there may be a shower coming. Put your flowers in the trug, Aunt Sophie, and let's hurry along into the house and put on our bonnets. We must set off to deliver these flowers to Mrs Wilder before it starts to rain.'

Sadness crept over Felicity as they neared her old home near Hertford. She noted every familiar landmark as they drove through the village she knew so well as a child.

She remembered with tender feeling her parents and past friends until the carriage swept up before the manor house.

His lordship had chosen to ride ahead of the coach and had arrived a little before Felicity and her aunts. He was talking to Augustus in the house when the coach came to a stop by the front door. They came out on hearing the carriage, with Beatrice and the children.

Felicity's eyes were mainly on John, noting how tall and assured he appeared standing before the old house she'd known and loved all her childhood.

It seemed right that he should be there. He represented her good fortune having returned to her after she'd been cast out. He caught her attention. Did she see him wink? Anyway, his smile heartened her.

Her brother had grown decidedly plumper since Felicity had seen him last. He appeared less sure of himself and kept mopping his florid face with his lacy handkerchief, although it was not a hot day. What bothered him? Felicity wondered if it was his guilty conscience.

But it may just have been what Viscount Coombe had had to say to him. Certainly Aunt Sophie could banish any fears that Augustus would try and dominate his lordship. Augustus reminded her of a whipped cur.

Beatrice seemed to have lost a good deal of her youthful prettiness. Felicity thought her lined face showed her avaricious character, which looked so different from her aunts' benign looks.

Felicity felt sorry for the little children as Beatrice poked and spoke sharply to her two boys, and their baby sister, reminding them to keep quiet, and making them stand stiffly in a line ready to curtsy and bow to their aunt who was soon to be a member of the aristocracy.

Felicity felt an overwhelming urge to hug her chubby niece, and make her subdued young nephews laugh. Suddenly she knew she must forgive the hurt this side of her family had done her.

For the sake of these innocent children she wanted to be as kind to them as her aunts had been to her. She stepped lightly out of the coach with a smile for them all.

'I am pleased to be here again!' she said.

There was an unmistakable hint of jealousy on Beatrice's face on seeing the beautiful new gown she was wearing as she moved forward to kiss her sister-in-law.

'Why, Beatrice, what a sweet, little daughter you have! And such fine sons, too. I've been longing to meet them, and to see you again.'

This little speech pleased Beatrice.

Augustus walked up to kiss her, too, mumbling something about being glad to see her, but Felicity feared she'd embarrassed him by coming.

'What a delightful poppet you are!' Felicity cried, stooping to pick up the baby girl, whose little face became alight with merriment.

'And what's your name?' she asked as she smoothed the child's petal soft cheek with her finger.

'Pil-ipa.'

'And your brothers?'

'He's Wil-lam,' Philippa said, pointing her tiny finger at the tallest boy. 'And he's Georgie.'

'Well, I have brought Philippa, William and George a present each,' Felicity said. Gazing down at the two boys, still standing stiffly, she said to them, 'Your new uncle-to-be, John, helped me choose a present for you, so I'm hoping you'll like them. Shall we go and find them in the carriage?'

The unexpected surprise made the

boys grin and jump for joy. Their parents couldn't stop the whoops of delight as they raced to the carriage for their gifts.

Lord Coombe, with a distinct smile on his face, had strolled over to watch the boys take their long packages and unwrap their new fishing tackle.

'A dolly!' Philippa was thrilled as she cuddled her china doll and showed it to Felicity as though she'd never seen it before. They all thanked their Aunt Felicity excitedly.

'Sir,' the boys yelled, scampering up to his lordship whose well-muscled figure was able to take the lads' onslaught, 'please teach us how to fish.'

The tension soon left everyone as Augustus talked companionably to Lord Coombe as he led the boys down to the nearby river. Meanwhile, the ladies retired into the house.

'What an elegant house you have!' Aunt Jane exclaimed.

Beatrice looked relieved, and as

she continued to have compliments showered on her by her visitors, her nicer side emerged. To Felicity's amazement, her aunts began to chatter amicably and seemed to get on quite well together. And so it turned out to be a very pleasant day for them all.

When she left, Felicity felt that she would love to come and visit her family again. In fact, she felt that when she was married, she would very much like Beatrice and Augustus to bring their children to visit them. Felicity smiled proudly at John. She had a strong suspicion that he'd planned the reconciliation.

10

Having spent the night in Hertford, they set off early in the morning to make the long drive up the Great North Road towards Huntingdonshire. The carriage horses tossed their heads and trotted along the road as though they seemed to be enjoying their exercise.

'What pleasant weather it is!' Aunt Sophie exclaimed as she leaned forward to gaze out of the coach window at the expansive sky over the flat countryside.

The growing season was encouraging the tall meadow grasses and the spring wheat to shoot up rapidly.

'Oh, just look at those swans with their cygnets in the river!' Aunt Jane cried as they bowled over a bridge.

She seemed to be delighted to see the countryside away from London.

Felicity, too, felt the thrill of seeing

the newly-leaved oaks; birds busily foraging for their nesting material; yellow primroses and buttercups peeping from under the hedgerows.

But a growing apprehension clouded the day for her. She'd detected that even John seemed a touch sombre, and supposed it was the thought of introducing his intended bride to his difficult father.

They were to lodge at a superior inn, as the Earl of Wanstead had not invited them to stay.

John had explained that most of the rooms in the hall had been shut up since his mama died.

Fortified by a good lunch, the party set off to visit the earl soon after. From the porter's lodge, the drive wound through an extensive and attractive parkland, where cattle grazed or stood placidly under the shade of the park trees swishing their tails.

The house looked incredibly big compared with the much smaller houses Felicity was accustomed to.

Its solid Roman style was dignified, but a little forbidding. There was no one to greet them when they arrived outside.

'If you would be so good as to wait in the entrance hall, I'll find my father,' John said, dismounting and, calling in vain for a groom, he looked annoyed before he tied his horse's bridle up to the carriage.

'What a splendid house this is!' Felicity remarked, determined to maintain her good humour.

She twirled around looking at the huge flagged entrance hall, admiring the ornamental decoration of great swags of fruit and flowers.

'Well, it might be impressive, but it is not comfortable,' Aunt Sophie grumbled. 'There's nowhere to sit.'

Aunt Jane disappeared into a side room and called, 'Sophie, there are some chairs here in this salon.'

As Aunt Sophie went to join her sister, she said to Felicity, 'I can't think what has happened to John. Perhaps you can find a servant to bring us a drink. I'm quite thirsty after that long drive.'

Not finding a bell rope, Felicity set out to locate the kitchen. The interior of the great house was truly magnificent. The one thing it lacked, Felicity decided, was a woman's touch. It looked empty.

Although clean enough, it demanded bowls of flowers, children's toys, or possibly some evidence of the owners' interests lying about to bring some life into it.

Quite how she ended up wandering into a small, private sitting-room at the back of the house she did not remember. A dog growled.

'Quiet, Battle.' The man's deep voice sounded hushed. The thickset bulldog ignored the command, and barked again, and came trotting out from behind a screen.

'Get out! He doesn't like strangers!' the voice warned.

Felicity blinked behind her glasses.

The sturdy dog appeared quite amiable to her.

'There's a good boy,' Felicity said unafraid, and bending down, she patted the dog's wrinkled head and was rewarded with a slobbering lick.

As nothing but the dog's contented snorts could be heard, the voice sounded peeved.

'Who are you?'

'Miss Felicity Ward.' There was no point in curtseying as she couldn't see him. 'I'm very sorry to intrude, sir, but I was seeking a drink for my aunts.'

'What, more than one female has come?'

By this time Felicity had guessed by his grumpy tone who he must be. John had been right in his assessment of his father.

'There are only three of us, your lordship,' she said brightly.

She thought she heard him murmur something about three being too many.

'Well, you could hardly expect me to come unaccompanied!'

She decided she was tired of talking to a screen, and crept forward.

He must have heard her footsteps.

'Don't come any closer, girl!'

She froze. What mystery was this? Earl Wanstead was as bad as his son.

'If I am to marry your son, I must see you,' she reasoned out loud.

'I'm not much to look at.'

'Nor I, your lordship.'

He must have put his eye to a crack in the screen as she heard him give a low whistle.

'I'd say John's found a beauty!'

'I don't think you can see me properly, my lord. I'm not in the first flush of youth and have to wear spectacles most of the time. So there, you need not feel embarrassed to show yourself.'

Felicity heard him move.

'Don't say I didn't warn you!' he called out.

The man who emerged from behind the screen was tall, still handsome in his old age, but the fact that he had a patch over one eye, a red scar down one cheek, one empty sleeve pinned up and used a stick to hobble took her breath away for a moment.

'Are you a war veteran?'

'Got hurt at Badajoz, ma'am. Wouldn't have my son go through the same thing!'

Felicity smiled at him.

'Nevertheless, John is brave, too,' she said, recovering quickly from her surprise. 'And like your son, you also prefer to conceal things! Oh, indeed, you are very alike. And I suspect just as kind and forgiving.'

The earl was clearly taken aback at the shower of compliments.

'You have a lot to say for yourself, ma'am.'

'Indeed, my lord, we will have much to discuss, I'm sure. But shall we order tea first, for my poor aunts are parched.'

'Not in the house five minutes and you're already running the place, I see!'

163

Felicity laughed lightly and stepped up and kissed his scarred cheek.

'There now, my lord, you know us ladies bring a little comfort and joy into men's lives. Why else did you miss your dear wife when she died?'

'I can't deny you're right.'

'Do come along to the entrance salon and meet my dear aunts who are most agreeable, and are looking forward to meeting you.'

His lordship looked down approvingly at his future daughter-in-law.

'John told me you were a sensible woman. And so you are.'

Noises sounded from the doorway, and Felicity swung around and was delighted to see Lord Coombe had entered the room, and Battle had padded over to greet him.

Over the dog's yelps of joy the earl boomed, 'So there you are, my boy. Where have you been since you arrived? Felicity had to introduce herself.'

'Looking for you, Papa. And finding your butler to order some lemonade for the ladies. I thought you had fled the house to avoid us!'

'Nay, and Felicity says they prefer tea.'

'I'm sure my aunts will be just as pleased with a glass of lemonade, my lord,' Felicity interrupted.

The earl remarked, 'If your aunts are as easy to please as you are, my dear, then we should all do well together. Help me to get down to the salon, will you? Tell me, do they like a game of cards?'

'Indeed they do,' Felicity said, giving John a wink as he opened the door for them.

★ ★ ★

It was most satisfactory to find the earl liked Aunt Sophie and Aunt Jane as much as they seemed to like him.

As the trio enjoyed a walk in the gardens, an evening of cards was arranged.

Within a few days, the earl arranged

to spring clean a few bedrooms so that the party could move into the Hall.

While John excused himself to do some estate work for his father, Felicity kept herself occupied because the housekeeper asked her advice about what dishes to cook.

'Here's to you, Felicity,' the earl said as he lifted his glass of wine having finished his dinner one day. 'Since you came, the cook has been providing us with some delicious meals.'

'I'm glad you like them,' Felicity said, flattered.

The earl turned to his son.

'You have a treasure,' he said.

John smiled at Felicity in a way that made her even more sure that he was still hiding something from her.

One day, Felicity had been asked to check some of the household linen with the housekeeper, which came easily to her as she used to do the same at her father's manor before he died and she was told to leave.

'We staff do like having you here,'

the housekeeper told her. 'This house is so big it needs a family in it.'

'You are all so efficient,' Felicity said. 'It is a shame you normally have so little to do.'

'I heard a whisper that the earl is thinking of moving into the Dower House, so perhaps you will come here when you are married, ma'am. It would be nice to have you here, and children around the place.'

Felicity wasn't sure it would be that kind of marriage. She already had it in her head it was a marriage of convenience and she hadn't quite convinced herself that he didn't have a mistress tucked away somewhere out of sight.

Determined to find out, she began to question the servants to find out where his lordship went each day.

'Now let me see, ma'am,' the butler said, his bland face polite and not showing what he thought of the lady's curiosity. 'The day before yesterday he was in the estate office going over the accounts with the earl's agent. Took them all day, but it was raining so they couldn't do much else.

'Yesterday morning he rode over to supervise the sheep market. And in the afternoon he went to the village to see which cottages needed rethatching.

'This morning, I believe he's gone to overlook the cutting of the rushes around the park lake. It gets a bit clogged up this time of the year unless they're cut back, ma'am.'

'Has Lord Coombe any friends he visits around here?'

'Oh, yes, ma'am. There's the Longford family, and Sir James and his wife, and then there are his school and university friends, Toby Wild and — '

'Thank you, Williams.' The list seemed never-ending.

Felicity realised she was not going to find out anything she wanted to know from this discreet fellow.

Probably all the hall servants would be tight-lipped about their master, and so they should be.

★ ★ ★

In the quietness of her bedchamber that evening, Felicity questioned her maid.

'Bet, I was wondering if you had heard any of the servants talking about Lord Coombe's friends. Has he any female friends living near here, for example?'

Bet's face looked surprised.

'Can't say that I have. Do you want me to try to find out?'

Bet and Tom had become very close of late, and Felicity expected they would marry one day.

'Well, I would like to know. When I am married it would be nice for me to have some lady friends.'

'Yes, miss.'

That evening, John came up to her side after dinner. His eyes intently upon her he said, 'Felicity, I have at last finished all the estate work my father had asked me to do for him. I am now determined to have my heart's desire.'

169

'Indeed, and what is that, my lord?'

'Take my arm and let us stroll around the lake, for the evening is fine, and it will take some time for me to explain.'

Felicity found walking arm-in-arm was as delightful as dancing with him. They did not talk as they strolled out of the house and out through the formal gardens, inhaling the sweet aroma of the box hedge.

He took a deep breath.

'I understand,' he urged her to slow her steps, 'that while I have been looking over the estate, you have been doing a fine job in the house. The housekeeper tells me that the linen had not been checked for years, and mending has been done. That was most kind of you.'

Felicity smiled up at him.

'I've been enjoying myself. I used to keep house for my father. But now the task is over I don't know what I shall do next.'

His hand slipped into hers as they

reached the shrubbery out of sight of the house.

'I don't think you need to worry about that. We are to wed.'

They strolled on until they were overlooking the lake. She looked into the distance with only one thought. Being with John was a pleasure. The evening light on the lake added a romantic aura.

'Yes, we are to wed,' she repeated, her heart hammering with the feeling that she longed to be truly his, or was she? 'John, I must ask you, do you have a mistress?'

'Most certainly not! Whatever gave you that idea?'

Her face burned with embarrassment at her bluntness.

'You are keeping something from me, I can tell.'

'Dear heart, I promise you I don't keep a woman in my closet, no matter what my valet may have told you.'

So he had heard that she'd been questioning the servants! Felicity found herself going a deeper red.

'For heaven's sake, John, I believe you are telling the truth. But I do believe that you've been keeping some other secret from me. I won't marry you unless you bare your soul!'

He rubbed his chin and scratched his eyebrow with one finger as though trying to think.

The crimson sunset light shone on the lake and she began to wonder if she had imagined he had a secret that didn't exist, like a mistress.

'Well, I wasn't going to tell you,' he began, and her eyes darted to his to hear his confession. 'I regret to say that I intended to cheat my papa.'

'John! Whatever for? He is old and has been terribly injured.'

'Yes, yes, I know. But growing up with only him and no mother was very hard. He forbade me to join the army which I dearly wished to do. Then he ordered me to marry and beget an heir, and so I thought I would marry . . . and not beget an heir.'

'Oh!'

He put his arms around her, then lifted her chin with his finger so that he could gaze steadily into her eyes.

'But, I can't do that. My plan to get my revenge on him will not work.'

'How so?'

'Because I happen to have fallen in love with the girl I want to marry. I want to experience all the joys marriage has to offer.'

A gurgle of laughter escaped Felicity.

'It is just as well that I love you!'

'Yes, indeed it is.'

She snuggled up to him.

'Is there anything else you have kept hidden from me that I should know about?'

'Perhaps there is one more thing . . . look!'

She gave a slight tremble as he placed a small box in her hands.

'Oh, dear, what is this?'

Apprehensively she opened it. Inside sparkled a blue sapphire brooch.

She felt tears in her eyes.

'It's the missing piece from my set of jewels, isn't it? How clever of you to find it.'

She stood on tip-toe to kiss his lips sweetly.

He took the brooch and as he pinned it on her dress in the centre he said, 'I admit it was not easy to find. It took Tom and I some time to search for this missing piece of jewellery. Augustus helped us. He even insisted on paying the owner an enormous sum to get it back for you, and I did not argue. He owed you that.'

Felicity's lips reached up to his for a kiss. He did not keep her waiting. Knowing she now had her heart's desire, she murmured, 'I couldn't be happier.'

'Nor I,' he said quietly before kissing her again.

Other titles in the
Linford Romance Library

SAVAGE PARADISE
Sheila Belshaw

For four years, Diana Hamilton had dreamed of returning to Luangwa Valley in Zambia. Now she was back — and, after a close encounter with a rhino — was receiving a lecture from a tall, khaki-clad man on the dangers of going into the bush alone!

PAST BETRAYALS
Giulia Gray

As soon as Jon realized that Julia had fallen in love with him, he broke off their relationship and returned to work in the Middle East. When Jon's best friend, Danny, proposed a marriage of friendship, Julia accepted. Then Jon returned and Julia discovered her love for him remained unchanged.

PRETTY MAIDS ALL IN A ROW
Rose Meadows

The six beautiful daughters of George III of England dreamt of handsome princes coming to claim them, but the King always found some excuse to reject proposals of marriage. This is the story of what befell the Princesses as they began to seek lovers at their father's court, leaving behind rumours of secret marriages and illegitimate children.

THE GOLDEN GIRL
Paula Lindsay

Sarah had everything — wealth, social background, great beauty and magnetic charm. Her heart was ruled by love and compassion for the less fortunate in life. Yet, when one man's happiness was at stake, she failed him — and herself.

A DREAM OF HER OWN
Barbara Best

A stranger gently kisses Sarah Danbury at her Betrothal Ball. Little does she realise that she is to meet this mysterious man again in very different circumstances.

HOSTAGE OF LOVE
Nara Lake

From the moment pretty Emma Tregear, the only child of a Van Diemen's Land magnate, met Philip Despard, she was desperately in love. Unfortunately, handsome Philip was a convict on parole.

THE ROAD TO BENDOUR
Joyce Eaglestone

Mary Mackenzie had lived a sheltered life on the family farm in Scotland. When she took a job in the city she was soon in a romantic maze from which only she could find the way out.

NEW BEGINNINGS
Ann Jennings

On the plane to his new job in a hospital in Turkey, Felix asked Harriet to put their engagement on hold, as Philippe Krir, the Director of Bodrum hospital, refused to hire 'attached' people. But, without an engagement ring, what possible excuse did Harriet have for holding Philippe at bay?

THE CAPTAIN'S LADY
Rachelle Edwards

1820: When Lianne Vernon becomes governess at Elswick Manor, she finds her young pupil is given to strange imaginings and that her employer, Captain Gideon Lang, is the most enigmatic man she has ever encountered. Soon Lianne begins to fear for her pupil's safety.

THE VAUGHAN PRIDE
Margaret Miles

As the new owner of Southwood Manor, Laura Vaughan discovers that she's even more poverty stricken than before. She also finds that her neighbour, the handsome Marius Kerr, is a little too close for comfort.

HONEY-POT
Mira Stables

Lovely, well-born, well-dowered, Russet Ingram drew all men to her. Yet here she was, a prisoner of the one man immune to her graces — accused of frivolously tampering with his young ward's romance!

DREAM OF LOVE
Helen McCabe

When there is a break-in at the art gallery she runs, Jade can't believe that Corin Bossinney is a trickster, or that she'd fallen for the oldest trick in the book . . .

FOR LOVE OF OLIVER
Diney Delancey

When Oliver Scott buys her family home, Carly retains the stable block from which she runs her riding school. But she soon discovers Oliver is not an easy neighbour to have. Then Carly is presented with a new challenge, one she must face for love of Oliver.

THE SECRET OF MONKS' HOUSE
Rachelle Edwards

Soon after her arrival at Monks' House, Lilith had been told that it was haunted by a monk, and she had laughed. Of greater interest was their neighbour, the mysterious Fabian Delamaye. Was he truly as debauched as rumour told, and what was the truth about his wife's death?

THE SPANISH HOUSE
Nancy John

Lynn couldn't help falling in love with the arrogant Brett Sackville. But Brett refused to believe that she felt nothing for his half-brother, Rafael. Lynn knew that the cruel game Brett made her play to protect Rafael's heart could end only by breaking hers.

PROUD SURGEON
Lynne Collins

Calder Savage, the new Senior Surgical Officer at St. Antony's Hospital, had really lived up to his name, venting a savage irony on anyone who fell foul of him. But when he gave Staff Nurse Honor Portland a lift home, she was surprised to find what an interesting man he was.

A PARTNER FOR PENNY
Pamela Forest

Penny had grown up with Christopher Lloyd and saw in him the older brother she'd never had. She was dismayed when he was arrogantly confident that she should not trust her new business colleague, Gerald Hart. She opposed Chris by setting out to win Gerald as a partner both in love and business.

SURGEON ASHORE
Ann Jennings

Luke Roderick, the new Consultant Surgeon for Accident and Emergency, couldn't understand why Staff Nurse Naomi Selbourne refused to apply for the vacant post of Sister. Naomi wasn't about to tell him that she moonlighted as a waitress in order to support her small nephew, Toby.

A MOONLIGHT MEETING
Peggy Gaddis

Megan seemed to have fallen under handsome Tom Fallon's spell, and she was no longer sure if she would be happy as Larry's wife. It was only in the aftermath of a terrible tragedy that she realized the true meaning of love.

THE STARLIT GARDEN
Patricia Hemstock

When interior designer Tansy Donaghue accepted a commission to restore Beechwood Manor in Devon, she was relieved to leave London and its memories of her broken romance with architect Robert Jarvis. But her dream of a peaceful break was shattered not only by Robert's unexpected visit, but also by the manipulative charms of the manor's owner, James Buchanan.

THE BECKONING DAWN
Georgina Ferrand

For twenty-five years Caroline has lived the life of a recluse, believing she is ugly because of a facial scar. After a successful operation, the handsome Anton Tessler comes into her life. However, Caroline soon learns that the kind of love she yearns for may never be hers.

THE WAY OF THE HEART
Rebecca Marsh

It was the scandal of the season when world-famous actress Andrea Lawrence stalked out of a Broadway hit to go home again. But she hadn't jeopardized her career for nothing. The beautiful star was onstage for the play of her life — a drama of double-dealing romance starring her sister's fiancé.

VIENNA MASQUERADE
Lorna McKenzie

In Austria, Kristal Hastings meets Rodolfo von Steinberg, the young cousin of Baron Gustav von Steinberg, who had been her grandmother's lover many years ago. An instant attraction flares between them — but how can Kristal give her love to Rudi when he is already promised to another . . . ?

HIDDEN LOVE
Margaret McDonagh

Until his marriage, Matt had seemed like an older brother to Teresa. Now, five years later, Matt's wife has tragically died and Teresa feels she must go and comfort him. But how much longer can she hold on to the secret that has been hers for all these years?

A MOST UNUSUAL MARRIAGE
Barbara Best

Practically penniless, Dorcas Wareham meets Suzette, who tells her that she had rashly married a Captain Jack Bickley on the eve of his leaving for the Boer War. She suggests that Dorcas takes her place, saying that Jack didn't expect to survive the war anyway. With some misgivings, Dorcas finally agrees. But Jack does return . . .

A TOUCH OF TENDERNESS
Juliet Gray

Ben knew just how to charm, how to captivate a woman — though he could not win a heart that was already in another man's keeping. But Clare was desperately anxious to protect him from a pain she knew too well herself.